Gnome Schooled

CLAW & WARDER
Episode 6

Erik Henry Vick

RATATOSKR PUBLISHING

NEW YORK

Copyright © 2020 by **Erik Henry Vick**

All rights reserved. No part of this publication may be reproduced, distributed or transmitted in any form or by any means, without prior written permission.

Ratatoskr Publishing
2080 Nine Mile Point Road, Unit 106
Penfield, NY 14526

Publisher's Note: This is a work of fiction. Names, characters, places, and incidents are a product of the author's imagination. Locales and public names are sometimes used for atmospheric purposes. Any resemblance to actual people, living or dead, or to businesses, companies, events, institutions, or locales is completely coincidental.

Gnome Schooled/ Erik Henry Vick. -- 1st ed.
ISBN 978-1-951509-08-8

TABLE OF CONTENTS

Chapter 1 1
Chapter 2 27
Chapter 3 183
Chapter 4 231
Chapter 5 243
AUTHOR'S NOTE 251
ABOUT THE AUTHOR 253

In loving memory of my nephew,
John Reid Grubba,
who passed away during the creation
of this novel.

I hope you enjoy *Gnome Schooled*. If so, please consider joining my Readers Group—details can be found at the end of the last chapter.

CHAPTER I

THE BODY

In the magical justice system, magically based offenses are considered bad form.

In the Locus of New York, the dedicated teams of supernatural detectives who investigate these breaches of Canon and Covenants are members of an elite squad known as the Supernatural Inquisitors Squad.

These are their stories.

I

Lori Caron grunted at the weight of the gray garbage bag as she shoved it out the door and into the alley behind her small restaurant. She shared a dumpster with a donut shop and magazine stand, and it stood forty yards down the alley. She groaned at the smell of the brick alleyway, sneering at the loose trash, the empty boxes.

She'd gone half the way to the dumpster when she saw the worn ankle boots sticking out from underneath a stack of wet cardboard. She heaved a sigh and dropped her garbage bag. "Miss?" she called. "You can't sleep here."

The woman didn't answer, didn't even *move*. Lori sucked her teeth and glanced down the alley toward Franklin Street. It was late—too late for foot traffic—and she was more than a little wary of waking someone up who wanted to sleep under wet cardboard in an excrement-scented narrow brick-paved passage.

"Ma'am?" she yelled, walking toward the booted feet. She nudged one of the boots with her toe. The foot flopped sideways, exposing a tiny silver wing embossed in the boot's side.

Other than that there was no reaction. "Hey, listen, I know where there's a shelter where you can get cleaned up, get a hot meal. I'll even give you an extra-large coffee to keep you warm on your way over there." She peeled back the top layer of cardboard. "But you really shouldn't sleep here. This alley is narrow, and the garbage trucks squeeze down here to get this dumpster. They literally scrape the walls with their fenders. It's not safe." She peeled back the next layer of cardboard and gasped, her hand flying to cover her mouth.

The boots contained the pale-skinned legs of an angel. A *dead* angel. Her once-ivory wings had faded to a dull, lifeless gray beneath her, and her golden eyes had dimmed to a decrepit almond color. Her marvelous white-blonde hair had already begun to fall out and lay in tufts around her head.

Orange dust caked her nostrils and powdered her pale cheeks and upper lip.

With a face made ugly by wrinkles of disgust, Lori turned and trotted back to her restaurant to call the police.

2

Dru came back into the living room holding a couple of brews and handed one to Leery. She smiled at her mother and father, who sat across from Leery on the other couch. "Are you sure you won't have anything?" she asked.

"No, no," said Agrat. "Coffee this late gives me heartburn."

"It's all about training your stomach, I've found," said Leery.

Agrat smiled at him. "You do seem to…um…*train* hard."

Leery grinned. "I can't get enough of the stuff. Maybe it's being a cop, or maybe it's something to do with all that coffee in the Pack meetings, but I've gotten so I feel sort of naked without a coffee in my hand."

"Yes, well…" said Hercule, looking away.

"It's about time for the new Grand Cynosure's press conference," said Dru. She sat next to Leery and picked up the remote. "I wonder what all the hubbub is about this time."

"No doubt there will be more taxes," grumped Hercule.

"Or another census." Agrat smiled at Dru. "It seems knowing everyone's true identity has become so important of late."

Dru shrugged and grinned. "I got tired of dancing around it."

Hercule's mouth turned down at the edges. "I shall have words with that…that…*mosquito!*"

"I'll come with you," said Leery with a feral grin. "I've got a thing or two to say to that snarky bastard myself."

"Well, I can assure you, Jeffery DeRothenberg's lineage is not in question, but you're welcome to stand as my second." Hercule waved his hand. "This thing, these bad feelings between our two groups, it's enough. We should embrace one another. After all, both of our kinds lost the war."

"I like the way you think, Hercule," said Leery.

"Daddy, there's no reason to make a fuss," said Dru.

"A fuss? No reason to make a fuss? I shall not *abide a…a…a* leech *like DeRothenberg showing you such disrespect!* I shall—"

"Shh," said Agrat, swatting his arm. "His Eminence is taking the podium. Turn it up, Dizzy."

Dru clicked off the mute, and they all stared at the newly-sworn Grand Cynosure as he took the podium, the cast bronze pentagram of the Covenancy hanging from the black velvet curtains behind him. He climbed up on the box that lent him the height to see over the podium, tapped the microphone with a sharpened, claw-like fingernail, and cleared his throat. He took a moment to lick his palm with his long black tongue and use his viscous saliva to slick down the wispy white hair that danced on the crown of his head. The tips of his pointed ears twitched at a whine of feedback, and he tugged at his long white beard.

"I simply cannot believe the entities in our great Covenancy elected a *Redcap*!" snarled Hercule.

"He renounced that association, dearest," said Agrat in a long-suffering tone. "He's just an ordinary goblin now. And besides, the Redcaps are just an ethnic pride group."

"Hmph. Ordinary goblin, indeed!"

The Grand Cynosure cast his all-black, beady-eyed gaze directly at the camera and licked his lips. "My fellow supernaturals, citizens of the Covenancy, in case you've been in a coma these past months, I am Fidonk Slypinch, and I am your Grand Cynosure," he began. "As a collection of entities, we face a grave danger. A danger *most* grave," he said. "Yes, and as with all grave dangers, this one is most banefully hazardous. It is true. The Covenancy was once a place rife with opportunities for all supernatural kind. It was like a dream. A great dream. A delightsome fancy. A figment of awesome beauty. Yes." He gripped the edges of the podium, nodded, and rocked forward on his toes. "Yes, I said 'was once,' for it is no more! No, don't take to Twitter to tell me I'm wrong, for I am not! No! I know things, citizens of the Covenancy. Arch eruditions of the cloistered and covert variety. *Secret* things. Yes, fellow mystical beings, I, and I alone, can see the entire tapestry. You would do well to heed my words."

"If only he'd use those words to actually say something," grumbled Leery, slurping his coffee.

"Shh," murmured Dru.

"This peril we face"—Slypinch shook his head sadly—"this trouble that presents itself as a triviality, this mournful menace..." Again, his beady eyes stared into the camera. "It must not be allowed to grow unchecked! We must band together and stamp out our common foe! No, magical beings. I say, no! We must not turn a blind eye to this threat, this thing that snares so many of our youth, this susceptibility to distressful exposure! No!" The Grand Cynosure drew in a deep, hissing breath. "Yes, it is true! No. We must not allow this thing to go on unopposed. And for that reason, on this very day, I directed the Covenancy agencies of justice to create a network of togetherness and group one with another, bound by a common cause, dedicated to working side-by-side in order to stamp out this menace. Yes, mark your calendars, as history will no doubt record this as a *great day* in the long tale of supernatural kind. It shall be remembered as the *greatest of grand acts* of my administration. Mark my words, entities of power and entities of low birth, alike. Remember what I've said tonight!" He nodded at the camera, then rocked back on his heels, smiling. "I will take a few *relevant* questions from the press, but do not make it awkward as you did during my campaign, or I will leave."

"Uh..." said Leery.

"Yes, you in the front. Yes, yes, the fairy with the red hair. You look intelligent in your gossamer gown and sparkly sparkles. What, my dear, would you have me explain to you?"

"Uh, yeah… Thank you, Your Eminence. I'm Aoife ó Briain, of SNN. My question is a simple one. What—"

"Then, by all means, young Aoife, ask it. Ask it, and I shall educate you."

"Uh, yes. What is the danger as you see it?"

Slypinch reacted as if she'd thrown water in his face and stumbled a step back. His pale gray skin went pink as it flushed with anger. "I would've thought better of a lass from the Emerald Isle!"

"I'm from Minneapolis, and I mean no offense, Your Eminence. It's just that—"

"Well, deary, if you mean no offense, stop your foolish mouth. What is the danger, you dare to ask me? What could be so perilous as to demand a full-scale response as I've described?" He gripped the edges of the podium with white-knuckled fingers. "Well, I'll tell you! Illegal snacks and the vile creatures that create and distribute them!" He raised his blazing gaze from Aoife's face and glared around the room. "Surely, you all see it!"

The room filled with the susurration of low whispers, shuffling paper, and truth be told, a few guffaws.

"Oh, aye! Cheez-Its are diabolical! The gateway snack, they are, and our youth are tromping through that gateway by the thousands! Why, my own grandson can be found with the devilish orange dust 'round his nostrils most times of the day! Worse, still, I have notebooks full of reports of women who sit around their homes smoking the foul stuff while their children go hungry, their homes fall to disrepair and filth, and their husbands stray! And don't get me started on Hostess Fruit Pies! Or Cheetos! No, people of the Covenancy! No! We must not turn away from the ugly truths as I see them! We must not abide snacks a moment longer!" He brought his gaze back to Aoife and stared daggers at her. "There, my dear girl, I've answered your foolish question!"

"Um, thank you, Your Eminence."

"Your Eminence?" asked another reporter, a stone troll from the Rocky Mountain News.

"Yes?"

"Following up on Aoife's question…uh…can you tell us exactly who you've instructed to do exactly what?"

"Are you—" Slypinch froze, staring at the troll for a few moments. "Why, I—" He shook his head as if troubled by irksome mosquitos. "It's so perfectly clear—" His eyes grew wide, and his rubbery lips shook for a moment before he yelled, "Argh!" The Cynosure turned a grayish-red and stomped one foot. He flipped out his phone and fired off a text in a flurry of angry thumbs. "You…you…*idiots* have done it again! See if I take *any* questions next time!" He whirled the wrong direction and jumped down from his box, then spun around, confused for a moment, before spotting the door and tromping toward it.

"Your Eminence!" cried the troll. "I'm a huge supporter! I'm just…confused…" He trailed off as the Grand Cynosure stormed out of the room and slammed the door behind him.

"Well, I'm glad I watched that," said Leery in a sardonic tone. "I feel so enlightened."

Hercule snickered.

Leery opened his mouth to crack yet another joke, but both his and Dru's phones rang. "Uh-oh," he said, digging for his phone. "Both of them together usually mean one thing."

Dru swept into the kitchen and answered her phone.

Leery fumbled his phone out and accepted the call. "Oriscoe." He listened for a moment and craned his head to look at Dru. "Right. Be there in a few." He disconnected the call and turned back to Agrat and Hercule. "Sorry, folks. We're going to have to call this short. An angel gave up the ghost over in Tribeca."

"Sorry, Mommy and Daddy," said Dru as she came back into the room. "You can stay here if you'd like, but I'm not sure when we'll— *I'll*—be back."

"Our little baby is so important," said Agrat with a warm smile. "She's even called to investigate the death of *angels*, honey."

"More's the pity," said Hercule, but he smiled warmly at Dru.

3

Liz Hendrix was getting out of a cab as Leery bumped their cruiser up on the sidewalk, narrowly missing the cab's door. "Hey!" she yelled. "You almost took my leg off!"

Leery popped out, slammed his door, and held up his finger. "Ah, but I *didn't*. Do you have any idea how much control over a vehicle it takes to come that close and still avoid disaster?"

"Hi, Liz," said Dru over the roof of the cruiser. "You're wasting your breath. He's incorrigible."

"Yeah, I know," said Liz with a sigh. "Who watches the cops? No one, that's who."

"Is a dead set of wings what it takes to get you out of the crypt at this time of the evening, Your Grumpiness?" asked Leery.

Liz shook her head. "No, it takes a telephone. I take it you saw the speech tonight?"

"Saw it? Sure. Understood it?" Leery shook his head. "I don't think we're supposed to."

"You might be right." Liz paid the cabby and walked toward the entrance of the alley. "Come on. Dead angels don't last, and she's back this way. The Locus Cynosure, himself, called me out to take a look at her, so I want to see her *in situ*."

"Oh, fancy talk," said Leery. "I love it when you talk dirty."

Liz rolled her eyes and turned toward the two sergeants standing at the mouth of the alley—one man and one woman. They stood close together, whispering back and forth and smiling.

"Ilona, Gordon," said Leery with a nod. "Nice to see the both of you. How was Hotlanta?"

"Hot—" said Ilona.

"—but nice," said Gordon.

"Was your little hiatus from magic helpful?"

"Eh—" said Ilona.

"—you know how it is. All magic—" said Gordon.

"—all the time makes you too—"

"—reliant on the stuff. It's good to—"

"—swear it off now and again. You know—"

"—get up to date on the latest tech."

Dru chuckled brightly. "Oh, he definitely does *not* know that. Leery's a luddite for all practical purposes."

Ilona smiled at Dru, and Gordon leered at Leery. "Keep that up—" said Gordon.

"—and you'll end up drowning—"

"—in the stuff when you have to use it."

"It's cute," Leery said, "this little back and forth thing you've got going. Finishing each other's thoughts, I mean."

"Eh—" said Gordon.

"—it's a living," finished Ilona. She handed her clipboard to Dru, who signed in and handed it to Leery.

He looked down at the pen as if he'd never seen one. "What is this thing? Where's my quill?"

"Funny, blockhead," said Dru.

Leery scribbled his signature and handed the clipboard to Hendrix. He smiled at the sergeants as he stepped past them. "Stay safe, you two. Don't get tongue-tied."

"Funny—" began Ilona.

"—but not really," finished Gordon.

Leery chuckled and walked toward the spray of brilliant white lights set up down the crowded alley. A man stepped out of the shadows about halfway down the alley, and Leery nodded at him.

"Cofy," he said.

"None of that mess, Oriscoe."

"Hey, I was just kidding around, Iced."

The man sneered at him. "I've told you before, furball, my name is '*Ice*,' not Iced."

"Ice Cofy? You must be mistaken. There's no such abomination as 'ice coffee.' Everyone knows it's iced coffee that is going to lead to the apocalypse. I mean, ice coffee isn't even grammatically correct." He shook his head, curling his lip. "You need an editor, man!"

The wizard growled. "My name is *Ice Cofy*, and it has nothing to do with the *drink*!"

Leery cocked an eyebrow at him. "Hey, whatever. I'm just trying to help."

Cofy turned to Dru. "How can you stand it?"

"He's not so bad, once you get to know him...and always carry earplugs."

"Ouch," said Leery. "What are you doing here, Ice? The vic was an angel, not a ghost. Well, I mean...she's a ghost *now*, but before—"

"Right, but I'm not here because of the victim."

"No," said a deep, gravelly voice from the shadows. A giant stepped into the pool of light. He had a golden badge clipped to a chain around his neck, and it hung eight feet from the greasy bricks.

"Chief," said Dru.

"Nogan," he replied. "Or do we all have to start calling you Your Grace from now on?"

"Nogan's fine. I'm not a princess here. I'm just a detective, Chief Magnussen."

Cofy looked at her from under bunched brows, his lips pursed. "I heard rumors about you."

Dru laughed.

"They're all true, Ice," said Leery. He turned toward the giant, looking up into the broad face. "What brings the Chief of D's out at this time of night? I mean, I get that the victim is an angel, and all, but—"

"Not that," rumbled Chief Magnussen. "Didn't you see the Grand Cynosure's speech?"

"Yeah, but what does that have—"

"It's the war on snacks, Oriscoe," said Cofy. "Snack abuse has reached epidemic levels, and the GC wants us to put a stop to it."

"War on snacks?" Leery glanced at Dru. "When did the GC talk about that."

She flapped a hand at him. "All the stuff about dangerous dangers and hazardous hazards. Plus the grouping together to work together in groups."

"Ah. Right." He turned back to the Chief of Detectives. "But still, what's that got to do with this case?"

Cofy jerked his chin toward Hendrix, who was on her knees next to the angel's corpse, lifting the sheet and looking down at the rapidly decaying form. "She overdosed on curdles, man."

"Curdles?"

"Yeah, ground-up Cheez-Its mixed with Cheetos powder, then emulsified into Cheese Whiz and Velveeta. They bake it into bricks, then you either smoke it or grind it and snort it."

"That's cheesy," said Leery. When no one laughed, he sighed. "You see, I said—"

"Yeah," said the Chief. "We all heard it, Oriscoe. It's just not funny."

Leery pursed his lips, then looked at Ice. "So how do you know so much about this?"

"I used to work edibles, man."

"Ah. Then I guess you're here to look into the snack abuse angle?"

"Naw." Ice shook his head. "I'm teamed up with you two on this one."

Leery shook his head and opened his mouth, but the Chief of D's cut him off. "None of your nonsense, Oriscoe. This decision was made above your paygrade—heh, it was made above *my* paygrade. This comes straight from the commissioner, who got it from Locus Cynosure Endymion, who got it from the GC. So, you see, you have nothing to say about this after all."

"Uh, right. Like I said, welcome to the team, Ice," said Leery.

"Listen up, all of you," said Chief Magnussen. "This one needs to be solved quick-like. People are watching. Big people. This is the first case under the GC's new edict, and he wants it wrapped up successfully. And yesterday. Your instructions are to find the dealer who sold this angel her curdles, find his supplier, *and* locate the manufacturer. The GC has already said that if we don't handle this case to his satisfaction, he will take this case away and prosecute it in Covenancy court."

"Right. We either do what he wants, or he's going to take his ball and go home," said Leery.

"That's it exactly," said the Chief.

"Not for nothing, but we do homicide, Chief."

The giant nodded. "That's why Cofy is with you. Rely on his expertise, his contacts in the snack scene."

Leery nodded to Ice. "Sure thing, Chief."

"Then I'll leave you to it." The giant turned and walked toward the mouth of the alley. "Oh, and, Oriscoe?" he said, turning back.

"Yeah, Chief?"

"I want to be copied in on the important bits."

"Can do, boss."

Leery turned back to Cofy. "Coffee, Cofy?" he asked.

"Cute, furball. Cute."

"Hey, I'm trying to be polite. Anyway, all good police work happens when you have a cup of joe in your paw."

"Better be careful, or the GC might add coffee to the list of banned snacks."

Leery grimaced and knotted his eyebrows at Cofy. "Now, that's just hurtful, Ice."

"Besides, we better wait on the ME," grumped Ice.

4

Fifteen minutes later, Liz Hendrix dropped the sheet back over the smoking form of the dead angel and got up with a grunt. She walked back to Dru, Leery, and Ice, shaking her head and pulling off her gloves. "Well, it's definite," she said. "Cause of death is cheese-substitute overdose."

"No chance it was something else? Lightning?"

"Lightning?"

"Yeah," said Leery. "I hear the Big Guy upstairs is fond of lightning when his angels step out of line. I'd think snorting curdles would qualify."

"No," said Liz. "No lightning. Cheese-substitute overdose, like I said."

Leery shrugged.

"I had to work fast. Angels go to dust faster than a vampire with his cork pulled, and angel dust *is* addictive, after all. I've got samples, and I'll run the tests, but I'm one hundred percent sure on the COD."

"Get a sample of the curdles?" asked Ice.

"I did," she said. "I'll run a spectral analysis when I get back to the lab. Results will take a few hours."

Cofy nodded. "Check for mozzarella." Leery cocked an eyebrow. "Sometimes they use that instead of Velveeta."

"But mozzarella is wholesome food."

Cofy shrugged. "These cheese addicts don't care, man. And the guys making it will use anything on hand to cut all that orange with. You wouldn't believe some of the recipes I've seen."

"Why mozzarella, then?"

"I know of a crew that gets mozzarella from a local pizza shop owner as partial payment for protection."

"Ah. Gang?"

"Yep. Gnomes, too." He made a disgusted noise and frowned.

"As bad as Svartalfar and leprechauns?"

"Oh, hell yes," said Ice. "Gnomes are cute, see, and they run around in their little hats and matching outfits casting charms on all the girls. Dangerous thugs, though. Dangerous thugs."

"What's the name of the gang?" asked Dru.

"The Gardeners is the one I'm thinking of, but there's also Nomes, Noldor, Earthmen, Little Gray Men, to name a few."

"So many?"

"Yeah," said Cofy with a sigh. "Too many."

"Who else is in the snack trade?" asked Leery. "Not the zees, right?"

"Oh, sometimes you'll find a Zombie mafia family dealing a little, but they usually stick to the soft stuff. Taffy, Twinkles, like that."

"Then no curdles?"

"The leprechauns invented the stuff, and they still sling it. Some Svartalfar gangs, too. It's not really a zee kind of thing."

"Good," said Leery. "I'm a little tired of the undead."

Dru cleared her throat.

"Present company excluded," Leery said with a weak grin.

Dru patted his arm. "It's okay. I'm not really undead anyway, I just like making you squirm."

Liz coughed and turned her face away to hide her grin.

Cofy's gaze bounced back and forth between Leery and Dru. "Hey," he said, "you two a couple or something?"

"Nah," both Dru and Leery said at the same time and then laughed.

"No skin off my back, either way." Cofy glanced at Liz. "So, check for mozzarella or other cheeses. Maybe it'll help us nail down who she bought from."

"Right," said Liz. "I'll head out unless you have other questions?" She glanced at Cofy. "And send me other cutting agents, if you think of anything promising."

"Did she have ID?" asked Dru.

Liz nodded. "Yeah." She dug through the handfuls of evidence bags she'd collected and handed one to Dru. She also handed a polaroid of the angel to Leery.

"Oh, no!"

"What? You know her?" asked Leery.

Dru nodded. "Raguel."

"Sorry," said Leery with a shrug. "I'm half-Catholic, but..."

"She watches—*watched*—over the behavior of angels," said Cofy.

"Who watches the watchers?" asked Leery absently. "How did you know her, Dru?"

"Historically, the rulers of Gehenna are considered fallen angels. She came to visit from time to time, ostensibly to inspect Gehenna, but mostly it was a vacation from all that...*righteousness*. She hated it."

"Well, she sure underscored that point," said Leery.

"Come on," said Dru. "Let's get to work."

"Right," said Leery. "Where to first, Ice?"

"Let's head over to the Thirteenth Precinct edibles squad and talk to a cop I know. Get a gang sitrep—that's where the Gardeners are based, the Thirteenth."

"Ten-four," said Leery. "Hey, we can drop you, Liz."

"That's nice of you, but it's way out of your way."

"Not much. And plus, there's a Starbucks almost next door to your office."

"I should have known," said Liz with a laugh.

CHAPTER 2

THE INVESTIGATION

I

Ice Cofy had paled to the color of coffee with way too much cream, and his knuckles had blanched on the grab handle by the time Leery jerked the car up on the sidewalk to avoid a city bus, laying on the horn. In the back seat, Dru snatched at her handhold in the back, sliding this way and that.

"You're a *maniac!*" snapped Ice. "Where'd you learn to drive?"

Leery turned and tipped a wink at him. "I know I make it look easy."

"*Look out!*" Cofy cried, pointing out the windshield with his free hand.

Leery jerked the wheel to the left without taking his gaze off Cofy. "All it takes is practice."

Ice shook his head, then pointed out the front windshield again, mouth wide open, eyes wider.

"*Relax*, Ice. I've got this." Leery jerked the wheel back to the right, slewing the car into a partial skid, barely missing the rear end of another cross-town bus, then punched the accelerator to the floor. But at least he turned his head back to the front.

"Quit showing off, Leery, before I throw up," said Dru from the back seat.

Leery glanced at her in the rearview mirror. "Good thing we're here, then." He pulled the car into one of the angled spots in front of the building and hopped out, slamming the door behind him.

"He always drive like this?" asked Ice, slowly uncurling his fingers from the handhold. "I may have dented the Jesus-handle up here."

Dru chuckled. "If you did, it might have straightened out some of my finger-shaped dents in the thing. And to answer your question, no, he doesn't always drive like this. Today was a *good* day."

"That's good enough for you two, you're both immortal. Maybe I can drive from here on out?"

"Oh… I just assumed you were a Claw."

Ice opened his door and turned in the seat to swing his legs out. He peered back over the headrest at Dru. "Naw. I'm sort of unique in the whole force. I'm a summoner, so I'm my own Claw and my own Warder."

"Oh, that's interesting!" said Dru.

"Yeah. That's why I don't have a partner most of the time. Giving me a Claw is redundant, and giving me a Warder is dangerous because my eidolon will always put me first."

"I see. And do you have a favorite—"

"Are you two girls coming?" asked Leery from the precinct steps.

Ice smiled with half of his face. "He's a nut, huh?"

"You don't know the half of it, Ice," said Dru with a fond grin at Leery. "Come on, before he starts an argument with the desk sergeant."

They got out and strolled toward the steps.

"Everyone feeling better now?" asked Leery.

"I'll feel even better if you let me drive the rest of the day," said Ice.

"I don't think so, champ," said Leery. "I don't know you well enough."

"Yeah, I was thinking the same thing about you," said Cofy.

Leery shrugged. "So, who's your friend here?"

"A great detective by the name of Dawn Bogue. She'll know all about the gangs slinging snacks on the East Side." Ice tromped past him and pulled the door to the precinct house open. "Come on, I'll introduce you."

They followed him inside, down into the basement, and into the section of the building reserved for the supernatural police. He pointed at an old coffee machine. "Coffee's right there."

Leery arched his eyebrow at the old plastic machine, at the dust-caked pot. "Yeah…"

"Hey, it's cop-coffee anyway," said Ice. "It's not like having a clean machine is going to make it any better."

"You've got a point," said Leery, veering toward the machine. "The congealed grease might give it flavor, too."

"He'll literally drink anything, huh?" asked Ice.

Dru giggled. "You should see what he eats for lunch."

Ice glanced at Leery, who had gotten distracted by the sandwich vending machine. "No…"

"He figures the only thing that can kill him is magic and silver, so why not eat whatever's handy."

"So…he really is crazy then? The driving isn't just an act?"

"Just wait," said Dru, gazing at Leery warmly. "You haven't seen anything yet."

"Ice!" a woman squealed.

He spun around and smiled. "Hiya, Dawn. You're looking good."

"I *am* good, Ice, just like always." She came striding over from the other side of the room.

"Hey, meet Dru Nogan," said Ice. "I'm working with her and her crazy-ass partner, Leery Oriscoe." He hooked his thumb toward the vending machines.

"Delighted," said Dawn, cutting her gaze toward Leery. "Hey, he's not going to eat—"

"Yeah, he is," said Dru with a grin. "But he's Pack, so it won't hurt him a bit."

"Dawn's the best Claw I've had the pleasure of working with," said Ice. "She's a Nagual—a werejaguar if you like that better."

"Nice to meet you, Dawn. I'm a Warder."

"More than that, I think," said Dawn with a knowing grin. "I've heard stories about you."

"About me?" Dru arched an eyebrow.

"Sure, Princess."

Ice tilted his head to the side and cast a speculative look at Dru.

"My, but the rumor mill has been running in overdrive," said Dru. "But none of that 'Princess' or 'Your Grace' nonsense. In this realm, I'm just Dru Nogan."

"Right," said Dawn with a grin. "Anyway, I'm pleased to know you."

"Likewise."

"What'd I miss?" asked Leery, striding over, tuna salad dripping down his left hand, a mug of coffee sloshing in the other.

"And this escaped mental patient is Leery Oriscoe," said Ice. "Oriscoe, meet Dawn Bogue."

"She's a Nagual," said Dru. "And smart."

"Meetcha," grunted Leery around a mouthful of almost-green tuna salad. "Hey, your sandwich machine is much better stocked than ours."

"That's because no one in their right mind would buy crap from those machines," said Ice.

Leery shrugged. "More for me."

Shaking his head, Ice turned back to Dawn. "This isn't a social visit, Dawn. We need to pick your brain."

Dawn shrugged her shoulder. "What with the Grand Cynosure's speech and the new Locus directives, I figured as much."

"We've got a case," said Dru. "An angel who ODed on curdles."

"Oh, that's terrible!" Dawn glanced at Ice and nodded. "The Gardeners?"

"Yeah, maybe," said Ice.

"Come on," she said and turned to stride back across the room. "We can use the lieu's office. He's out of town."

"Still Lieutenant Camazotz?"

"Yep," said Dawn.

"I never liked him," said Ice. "Those creepy little eyes."

"Hey, he can't help it, Ice. He's mostly bat, you know."

"Like Batman?" asked Leery, grinning.

"Naw," said Ice. "Look him up on Google. Talk about a dark past."

"Oh, no," said Leery. "Every time I gargle I mess up the weather or the power or something."

Dru sighed and punched him in the shoulder.

"Hey, what's that all about?"

She arched an eyebrow at him and mouthed the word "gargle."

"Is my breath bad?" he asked. "I don't get it."

"Yes, you do." She turned back to Ice. "Ignore him."

"My pleasure," said Ice. "So, Dawn, what's the garden club up to? Still slinging cheese?"

"Oh, you bet. If anything, they're even more active than they were when you worked edibles. They've been expanding into LGM territory pretty heavily."

"I bet that doesn't sit well with the Big Gray Man."

"No, he's freaking out, to be sure. So far, with the Gang Unit's help, we've managed to keep it from erupting into World War III."

"No violence, then?" asked Dru.

"I didn't say that. Gnomes are mean bastards, especially to their own kind. Most people think goblins are the worst fae creature, but for me, gnomes win hands down."

"So, where can we find these ugly little jerks?" asked Leery.

"Depends on which set you want? The Gardeners run their operation out of Stuyvesant Town, just to the east of here. The Little Gray Men are in the Alphabets."

"Feel like taking a ride?" asked Leery. "Never hurts to have a familiar face along."

"Sure—"

"Dawn and I will take a separate car. You know, it'll look more impressive if there are two cars," said Ice. "Plus, it's probably easier on Dru's stomach if she rides up front."

Leery shrugged. "Suit yourselves."

"Where should we start?" asked Dawn.

"Well, we've got the ME checking for mozzarella in the curdle dust found on our victim, but she needs a few hours. Let's start with the Little Gray Men."

2

They followed Dawn and Ice down E 14th Street, and as they rolled through the intersection at Avenue A, Leery craned his neck, twisting his head this way and that. He put his foot on the brakes and slowed the car.

"What?" asked Dru. "As if I don't know."

"I was sure there was a Starbucks around here..."

"Remember when I showed you the Starbucks app?"

Leery grunted.

"You know what else you can do with it? Besides ordering your coffee in advance?"

"No idea. Gurgle stuff?"

Dru sighed. "No. But you can find all the Starbucks close by. Don't worry. There's one down across from Tompkins Square Park."

"Isn't that where Dawn said we were going?"

Dru nodded and said, "But on the Avenue B side. Evidently, the Little Gray Men hang out near the east playground."

"Ah." He looked longingly down Avenue A. "Are you sure that gizmo is right? I don't see a sign."

"Relax, Leery. The app is never wrong."

"That's what they say about grunge."

"*Google*, Leery! It's Google!"

"Nah, I meant the music style. They say it's never wrong, but try playing a little Soundgarden at a wedding reception. Everyone gets so pissed off."

"Sometimes, Leery Oriscoe, I'm not sure whether to believe you or not."

"Hey, they don't call me Honest Leery for nothing."

"Who calls you that?" Dru said with a grin.

"Well… There's…" Leery shook his head. "I'm sure someone does. Why wouldn't they?" He turned the car onto Avenue B. "Anyway, someone should have explained the priorities to Dawn."

"You mean to always park near the Starbucks?"

"*Exactly.* I knew you'd understand."

At the corner of 8th and Avenue B, Dawn pumped her brakes, turning her head from side to side, looking for a space. Leery sighed and pulled around her, hopping up onto the sidewalk near the entrance to the park and drove thirty feet along the paved path into the park. He killed the ignition and jumped out, pointing at the empty sidewalk behind him and waving Dawn in.

Instead of pulling in, Dawn rolled down her window. "That's not a legal space."

"Sure, it is. That's a cop car, right? That means wherever it's parked is a legal space."

Dawn's eyebrows bunched, but there were no other spots nearby, so she pulled up onto the curb and parked next to him. She and Ice got out, and she nodded her head toward the bunch of trees to the north of the playground. "They hang out in there, mostly."

"Right," said Leery.

The four of them turned and walked into the gloom, and somewhere in the trees, a piping voice yelled, "Five-O! Five-O!"

Leery sighed. "At least we don't have to identify ourselves."

In a small clearing, they found twenty or thirty gnomes standing in a rough circle, just inside a ring of mushrooms. Inside the circle, the grass had withered and died. Barefoot as they were, the gnomes were between twenty-four and thirty-six inches tall. They wore a lot of gray, though there was no uniformity in saturation or hue—some wore gray T-shirts, some gray conical caps, some gray pants, and all the myriad permutations of combinations.

"Stop right there, coppers," said one of the gnomes.

"Come on, Big Gray Man," said Dawn. "You know me."

"Right. I know *you*, kitty. I don't know these others." His narrowed gaze bounced from Ice to Leery, and then from Leery to Dru, where it locked on. "Oh. My. Word. Such beauty. You must be the Morrigan."

Dru smiled. "Not quite, but I bet you say that to all the girls."

"Only the beautiful ones. You can come into our ring if you wish."

"Thank you," said Dru, though she didn't move toward them. "So, are you the Big Gray Man?"

The gnome nodded with a sage air. "You can call me, Big G, or BGM. I don't stand on formality."

"Well, thank you, Big G," said Leery.

The gnome turned a fierce gaze on him. "You ain't pretty, so you can call me Mr. Man."

"Oh, is that your last name?" asked Leery.

"Never you mind, snoopy."

"You know, I'll take that from my friends—and my nemesis, of course—but from street thugs? Nah."

Big G cocked his head to the side, his pointed ears twitching. "Uh..."

"The dog name?" Leery grimaced when the little gnome continued to stare at him like he had three noses. "Snoopy?"

"No, idgit. I mean snoopy as in someone who likes to snoop in other people's business."

Leery glanced at Dru and shrugged.

"Listen here, BGM," said Ice. "You beefing with the Gardeners over turf?"

"Ha!" said the gnome. "Who told you that? The kitty?" He chuckled. "Those Gardeners are idiots."

"But they've taken a few blocks from you," said Dawn.

Big Gray Man shrugged. "Yeah, but we *let* them take those corners. They aren't profitable, and there's a fussy Neighborhood Watch around there. They keep calling the mundane cops, thinking we're drug dealers."

He cackled. "We made those dumb garden hoes think they were our best corners."

"Pretty good strategy," said Leery.

"Don't kiss up, wolfman," said the gnome.

"What do you know about curdles?" asked Dawn.

"Only everything there is to know," said Big G. "We invented it."

"No, you didn't. Everyone knows the leprechauns invented curdles," said Ice.

Big G glowered up at him. "Yeah? If you're so smart, why are you here asking me questions?"

"That's a good question if you're going to tell us lies."

Big G rolled his eyes. "Okay, fine. Yeah, we know about curdles, but we don't sell 'em—not anymore."

"And why's that, a big, tough crew like this?"

"We could if we *wanted* to," said another gnome.

"But we *don't*."

"Not even to pretty little angels being bad?" asked Leery. He held out the photo of Raguel's corpse.

"Oh, that's gross," said a short gnome standing at Big G's side.

"Curdled-brains are *annoying*," said yet another. "Especially the ones that can't handle it."

"Besides," said BGM, "curdles are old news. There's something much better, and since only a few gnomes know about it, the profits are crazy. Curdles, you gotta front for Cheez-Its *and* Cheetos, plus the jar of orange goop and the Velveeta."

"Yeah, and the curdle epidemic is why you can't buy those things in stores anymore," griped Leery.

"Right, right," said BGM.

"So, what's this other thing?" asked Ice.

"It's *legal*," said Big G. "No need to hassle us."

"I'm sure it is," said Leery. "For now."

"Right, so you won't mind if I don't tell you what it is."

"Peanut butter on cheddar," said Dawn with a grin.

"Also old," said Big G, but his expression colored him anxious.

"Oh, I know what you mean," said Ice. "Cookie butter, Nutella, and peanut butter on graham crackers."

The Big Gray Man's face fell. "No. That's not it at all."

"That's it," said Ice. "I read the bulletin on it last Friday," he said to Leery.

"Listen, Big G," crooned Dru. "If I wanted curdles, who should I see?"

"Me, babe," he said, puffing out his chest. "I'll make you a batch myself."

"Oh, that's sweet! But what if I want to buy it in quantity?"

"Ah." He released a pent-up breath. "The Gardeners still sling it. Leprechauns, of course," he said with a nod toward Ice. "So do the Earthmen and House Elves. I even think some of the bridge trolls are into it." He pursed his lips. "I think the Svartalfar got out of the trade."

"And do any of those have a signature cook? Like the Gardeners do with mozzarella?" asked Ice.

"Oh, sure," said BGM. "Every crew has their favorites. Leprechauns still cut it with ground-up Lucky Charms, of course. The Earthmen use parmesan. House Elves use tofu-based American cheese."

"And the Little Gray Men? What do you use?" asked Leery.

Big G squinted up at him. "You know, I don't think I like your attitude."

"I get that a lot."

"Come on," crooned Dru. "Tell us."

Big G shrugged. "We use macaroni and cheese powder. Sometimes the creamy gunk in the foil packs if we're low on Cheese Whiz, but mostly just the powder. You can buy it separately, now." He glanced at Ice. "But like I said, we don't make it anymore."

"Right." Ice grinned. "Don't worry, Big G, I'm not in edibles anymore."

"You've been super helpful," said Dru. "If you think of anything else, Dawn can get a hold of me."

"Yeah, but that could take time. What if it's an emergency?" Big G asked with a hopeful expression.

"Then you can call six-six-six like everyone else," said Leery. "Thanks for your help." He turned and led Ice and Dawn back toward the car.

"What if it's not…uh…police business?" asked Big G with a twinkle in his eye.

"Oh, honey," said Dru with a grin. "You wouldn't survive it." Giggling, she turned and followed Leery back to the others, who leaned against their respective cars, arms crossed. "Well, at least we have more information for Liz," she said.

"Yep. Could be helpful. The only trouble is, if everyone knows every other crew's secret ingredient and wanted to mix up a hot batch to get their competitors locked up, they could do that with no trouble."

"Yeah, but that's only if they *expected* us to assume it was a hit, and with all the Curdledbrains in this city, what's one more OD?" Ice shook his head. "Naw. I don't think they'd go to the trouble."

"Maybe not," said Leery. "Let me go call Liz and give her the other ingredients to look for."

"You do that," said Ice. "Me and Dawn are going to head to the Starbucks and grab a coffee. We'll meet you there."

"You really know how to hurt a guy, Cofy," grumbled Leery as he tapped in Liz's number. "I'll remember that about you."

"Serves you right, going on and on about my name being an abomination," Ice muttered as he swung into the car and slammed the door behind him.

Leery tossed the keys to Dru and got in the passenger side, his phone crooked against his ear. "Can't let him get all the good coffee, partner."

"Leery, we really need to talk about your addic—"

"Shh. It's ringing," he said.

3

Leery came out of the Starbucks carrying two *trenta*-sized cups of coffee and found Ice sitting behind the wheel with Dru in the passenger seat of their cruiser. "Well, that's not going to work," he grumbled. "There aren't any cup holders in the back."

"There aren't any in the front, either," said Ice. "Give me the keys, Oriscoe."

"There's Dru..." He quirked a grin and an eyebrow at Ice. "I thought you were riding with Dawn?"

"She had to get back to the precinct for a big briefing with the starched shirts from 1PP." Ice held out his hand. "Now, quit stalling and give me the keys."

"My hands are full."

Ice glanced at Dru. "Is he always this much of a baby?"

Dru quirked a smile at them both. "I hate to sound like such a broken record, but you have no idea. Don't ask him to Google anything."

"Tell you what, furball. Put one of those gallon jugs on the roof, fish out the keys and hand them over, then open the back door, grab your jug, and slide in. I'll get out and close the door so you won't need cup holders."

"What am I supposed to do? *Hold* these things the entire time?"

Dru laughed. "Come on, Leery. You make me hold them all the time. Besides, we both know one of those cups will be empty by the time Ice gets the car off the sidewalk and pointed in the right direction."

"So, you're against me, too." He sighed and slid one of the massive cups onto the roof. He fished out his keys and put them in Ice's waiting hand. "There. Happy?"

"Overjoyed. Get in the damn car."

When Leery was in he handed one of the cups to Dru and made a big show of getting his seatbelt on while Ice got out and closed the door, then he looked out the side window, pretending not to notice her holding the cup out. "What a nice day," he said.

"I *will* drop it in your lap."

Without looking, he retrieved his second cup of coffee. "Though, now it's looking a little overcast."

"What did Liz say?" asked Dru.

"She couldn't narrow it down yet, but the additional substance has a 'dairy profile,' whatever that means."

"That means we can cut down our circle of interest. Leprechauns use Lucky Charms, and that's definitely not dairy. House Elves use a tofu-based thing," said Dru. "That leaves the Gardeners and the Earthmen."

"Plus, anyone else who deals rock that BGM doesn't know about," said Leery.

"Gotta start somewhere," said Ice with a shrug. "Pick your poison."

"Aren't the Gardeners close by?"

"Gardeners it is." Ice turned the car north and drove them to Stuyvesant Town. "This set isn't like the Little Gray Men," he warned. "BGM likes to pretend they are a big-time tough crew, but they're small potatoes. The Gardeners aren't like that. Violence is a daily thing for them, and some of the gnomes don't distinguish things like cops or badges. All they see are gnomes and not-gnomes, so be careful."

"Right," said Leery, balling up the first *trenta* and tossing it onto the rear deck before flipping open the lid on the second cup.

Ice turned onto the First Avenue Loop, driving slowly and scanning for a parking spot.

"This is gonna be tough, finding a spot in the middle of the morning like this."

"Nah," said Leery sliding forward. He pointed at a little green Smart Car. "There's your spot."

"Yeah, that's a spot, but someone already in it."

Dru chuckled. "Slide out. I'll show you."

Ice shot his gaze back and forth between them for a moment, then got out when Dru nodded, and Leery followed suit.

"I taught her this, you know," said Leery.

Dru nosed the Crown Vic up to the bumper of the Smart Car, then applied the power. The car skidded and jumped toward the curb. Dru pumped the accelerator a time or two to get the front wheels of the Smart Car to hop up onto the sidewalk, then bulled the Crown Vic forward, pushing the little green car out of the way.

"I don't think you should brag about that." Ice turned as Dru hopped out and walked east. "Come on," he said. "The Gardeners like to hang out near the fountain."

Leery shrugged and took an enormous drag of coffee, then followed. As they headed down Stuyvesant Walk, he grinned at the calls of "PO-po" and "Five-O" that preceded them.

The shaded areas were full of gnomes, wood elves, dryads, and gremlins, all of whom followed the three cops with sullen gazes. Leery smiled and waved as though it were a parade. When they reached the Stuyvesant Oval—the concrete path surrounding the park—ten gnomes stepped from the woods. They were close to the same heights as the Little Gray Men, but their expressions were harsher, meaner, and they all seemed to wear a uniform of sorts: reddish-brown skin-tight leggings, a brown tunic covered in runes done in a thread that matched the fabric color, and conical red silk hats.

One of them stepped apart from the rest. "What do you want? We're paid up, and we aren't going to pay a higher rate, so you can just forget it."

"Paid up?" asked Leery, staring down at the gnome over the rim of his *trenta*.

"Never mind," said Ice. "Look, we're not here for a collection. Show him the picture, Leery."

"Right." Leery fished the polaroid out of his coat pocket and held it out. "You see this woman before?"

"Curdled-brains all look the same," he said after a cursory glance at the photo.

"Look again. This one's an angel."

"Yeah? So? We get all kinds coming down here, throwing their weight around"—he turned a cold glare on Ice—"making demands. You think I remember every face?"

"She ain't even a *gnome*," said one of the others with a curled lip.

"No, she *was* an angel, like I said." Leery stepped closer to the knot of gnomes and showed the picture again, staring into each gnome's eyes until the gnome glanced at the picture. "Anyone know her?"

"What's it to you?" demanded the one who'd spoken first.

"What's your name, player?" asked Ice. "I'm Cofy. Maybe some of your OGs mentioned my name."

"OGs?" asked Dru.

"Original Gnomes," said Ice without breaking eye contact with the gnome.

"Yeah, I heard of you. I'm Jenkor the Rake," said the gnome. "You hear of me?" He turned a sly gaze on Leery.

"Trust me, it's a good thing I haven't heard of you. I work homicide."

"Yeah," said Jenkor. He twisted his head toward Dru. "What about you, gorgeous? You hear of me?"

She shook her head. "I work homicide, too, though."

Jenkor nodded. "We haven't killed anyone, and none of the Gardeners are dead."

"Your crew still uses mozzarella in curdles, right?" asked Ice.

"The real stuff," added Leery.

Jenkor's eyes narrowed and flicked back to first Ice, then Leery. "We don't make curdles anymore. There's no profit in it."

"Don't give us that, Jenkor!" snapped Leery. "Everyone knows that if you want curdles on the Eastside, you come to Stuyvesant Town."

"Not anymore," said Jenkor, shaking his head. "The Little Gray Men—"

"Nah," said Leery with a chuckle. "We already talked to them. The Big Gray Man said we should come over here. He said your crew is on top of the heap."

"We *are*," said Jenkor, "but not because of that."

"Come on, Jenkor," said Dru. "We already told you we're homicide cops. We don't care who sells what except when it intersects one of our cases."

"Especially when it comes to snacks," said Ice. "They shouldn't even be illegal if you ask me."

Dru stepped closer, flashing a brilliant smile and cocking her head a little to the side, eyes sparkling. "Surely a big deal like you can help us."

Jenkor puffed up like an inflatable lawn decoration at Halloween. "I know some things," he said, sidling closer to Dru.

"Oh, I just bet you do," she crooned, turning up the wattage. "I bet you know all kinds of things." She took his hand and led him away from the rest of his crew, her voice dropping to a throaty whisper.

Leery stepped between the pair of them and the nine remaining gnomes. "Now, you punks listen up. Jenkor the Rake back there is going to help us out, and unless you want to spend some time beneath Rikers, so are you."

"Woah," said Ice. "Slow your roll, Oriscoe."

Leery glanced at him. "You take half, I'll take half. Let's see who scores points first."

"Loser rides in the back for the rest of the day."

"It's a bet."

"What if Dru wins?"

Leery grinned. "Then *she* rides in the back."

Cofy smiled and tapped five gnomes. "You fellas come with me." He turned and walked down the path.

The four remaining gnomes glared at Leery, hostile sneers decorating their faces.

"Right," said Leery, rubbing his hands together. "Who wants a get out of jail free card? We know one of your customers overdosed on some of *your* curdle dust last night. We *know* it came from you, and we have *evidence* to back that up. The first one of you who helps me out gets to go home, *and* he gets my business card decorated with the phrase 'Call Detective Oriscoe before booking.' I get that call, I come down and straighten things out for you on any non-violent crime."

The gnomes exchanged glances, but no one spoke.

"Hey, come on that's a good thing for little guys in your line of work."

"*Little?*" growled one of the gnomes.

"Hey, I didn't mean it like that. I meant guys at the bottom of the heap. The guys who do the real work but never get the expensive magisters when they get snatched up. The grubs."

"Oh, now we're bugs to you?" sneered one of them. "Denizens fit for the trash heap?"

"No, no. You're twisting what I'm saying. The drones. The drudges. The peons."

"Hear that, boys?" asked the gnome who'd spoken before. "We're *worthless workers*." He gave a nasty chuckle.

"Hey, I didn't mean it like that. I just mean that you guys are the foot soldiers."

The gnomes took a step forward, each face twisted with anger or disgust. "You frickin' talls are all the same."

"Hey, I'm a *trenta* man, myself. I think it's ridiculous calling a small cup a tall."

"What's that? Another size joke?"

Leery shook his head. "Come on, fellas. You're mistaking my meanings. All I meant was that surely a get out of jail free card could be helpful to you, okay? No size judgments involved."

"Right. You don't even see size, do you?" sneered the gnome.

Leery shook his head. "I…"

"Nothing else to say, *big* man?" asked the gnome.

"Hey, I chose the wrong words. I'm sorry, okay? Does that make you feel better? I'm an old fuddy-duddy who misspoke."

"You're an old something, all right," said the gnome taking a step closer.

"Right. Okay, I've had enough. You're all going in. Turn around, hands on your heads."

The gnomes leered at him, some giggling.

"Nope, man, I don't think so," said the gnome who seemed to be the leader. "You came in here, onto our turf, and only brought two others, and you think you're gonna throw your weight around?"

"Listen, you don't want to mess with the NYPD," said Leery. "And I'm a Claw, fellas. You know what that means." He leered at them ominously.

The speaker for the group tilted his head to the side and hit Leery with an appraising glance. He lifted his nose and sniffed the air. "Wolf," he said. "Don't you know you're standing in a gnome circle?" He stretched his arms wide. "This whole oval is our circle. Consecrated, man. You're not half as tough inside it as you are out."

Leery glanced at the edges of the path, looking for toadstools. "No mushrooms?" he said with a shrug.

"Shows what you know, wolf. That's the *old* way, and the Gardeners don't do anything the old way."

"Fine, whatever," said Leery. "Look, maybe I don't want the headache of writing up four arrest reports, okay? Help me out, and we'll call it a misunderstanding."

"I don't think so," said the gnome, taking another step closer. "Seems to me, you're like all those other arrogant coppers. Seems to me, you think you're better than us gnomes. Seems to me, you need a lesson in manners."

Down the path, Dru's bell-like laughter rang out, and he glanced in that direction. Jenkor sat in the palm of her hand, his legs crossed, bare feet resting on the inside of her forearm.

The four gnomes took another step closer.

"What's your name?" Leery asked the one who'd been speaking. "I'm Oriscoe."

"I'm Reknad the Machete," said the gnome.

"Listen, we got off on the wrong foot. Right, Reknad? Mistakes made on both sides. But we don't want things getting out of hand, do we?"

Reknad nodded and took a step closer. "Sure, man. We don't want no trouble." He waved and one of the gnomes with him turned and ran off into the trees.

"Right, me neither. I'm just doing my job. And right now—"

Reknad leaped at him, wrapping his arms and legs around Leery's left shin and climbing his leg like a tree trunk. The other two rushed forward, one lifting another so he could leap toward Leery's waist, then snaking up the back of Leery's leg like a monkey climbing a pole. The nimble gnome raced around his back, climbing upward with small jumps.

"Dammit," Leery mumbled as he kicked off his shoes. "This was a good suit."

The gnome hanging from his belt whooped and dug his bare feet into Leery's thigh, pushing off for another leap upward. As he did so, Leery let his wolf out in a rush, buttons from his shirt flying, his leather belt snapping. The gnome hanging from his waist leaped upward, grabbed the fur of his chest, and hung on. Leery grabbed at him, snarling as the little gnome's hand entwined in his chest hair and pulled.

Leery threw back his head and howled, and Reknad let out a loud whoop, then bit him in the knee. From the wooded park came answering whoops—and a lot of them.

"Oh, for the First of the Magi's sake!" snapped Ice. "*Haere mai, e taku tarakona, e taku hoa, aku kaiwawao!*" he chanted, throwing his head back and squeezing his eyelids shut. The gnomes he'd been talking to scattered as the air in front of him began to shimmer and shake with a sound like faraway thunder. An amorphous glob of bright golden light appeared in the middle of the shimmering air.

Leery pulled at the gnome clinging to his chest, ignoring the burning pain of a massive tuft of his chest fur coming away. The gnome thrashed in his palm, punching and kicking his taloned fingers, and Leery snarled at him. The gnome on his back reached around and pulled at his black woolen hat, blinking in confusion at the feel of Lucifer's charm beneath his fingers instead of fuzzy wool. Reknad jumped free and began to kick him in the shin, and Leery stooped and snatched him aloft by one arm, shaking him like a doll.

"*Ae, haere mai, he kaha. Haere mai ki taku awhina, tohea to mana,*" Cofy chanted as the golden, amorphous glob began to solidify, taking on a definite shape. Long golden limbs stretched from the center of its mass toward the ground, thickening and growing spikes and sharp edges as it did. Likewise, arms grew outward from its upper part, first two, then three, then another, two pairs of arms, joined at the shoulder. A lump formed at the top, heaving skyward with a slippery plop, forming a head and neck. Cofy snapped his eyes open, glaring at the gnomes he could see.

"Ssss-summoner," hissed from the golden creature, even as the light dimmed and its form began to harden, darkening to brushed bronze color.

"Atekhomen," said Ice.

"You called, and I came." The eidolon's voice sounded like molten copper dribbling into water, a series of plops and hisses and bell-like pings. "Who shall I kill? What shall I destroy?"

"Nothing and no one. Yet." Cofy glared at the gnomes gathering near the tree line. "Watch those gnomes."

"Very well," said the eidolon, though his tone said he didn't like it one bit. "Did you know there is at least a score of creatures coming this way through the trees?"

"Oriscoe! What the hell are you doing?" cried Cofy.

Leery's gaze snapped to his, and he snarled, shaking Reknad by the arm. The gnome trying to peel off his hat gave a grunting squeak as yellow-orange concentric circles slid down over his head. The rings tightened, snapping his arms to his sides, and he slid from Leery's shoulders.

Reknad bit him in the web of flesh between his thumb and forefinger, and Leery flung him away. The gnome crashed to the ground and rolled ass over teakettle to the line of trees. He got up shakily, glaring back at the wolf for a moment before turning to the gathered gnomes in the trees. "Follow me, gnomes!" He turned and charged back toward the sidewalk, twenty or so gnomes following in his wake, shouting war cries at the sky in piping little-boy voices.

Leery hurled the last gnome he held at the oncoming troop, snarling and showing his teeth. The gnome crashed into his compatriots, bowling some over. The others ran on, crying out and pointing at Leery.

Jenkor snarled something at Dru and jumped from her hand, landing on his feet and dodging one of her yellow-orange rune sets. He whirled and charged off into the woods.

"Now, Summoner?" asked Atekhomen. "Shall I rend and tear?"

"Contain them for now," said Cofy, striding toward Leery. "Watch my back."

"Certainly," said the eidolon in a disappointed tone. "I must say, in previous summons, you have allowed me to have much more fun. Can I at least *hurt* some of them?"

"If they leave you no choice."

Atekhomen sighed. "As you say." The eidolon strode toward the trees, throwing his arms wide and allowing chaotic magic to pour forth from his hands in a mad wave. Red fire erupted anywhere the wave of power touched the ground, sending flames leaping high into the air. The fire crackled as though fat dripped into it, and the gnomes danced back, throwing their arms up to shield their eyes.

"What happened?" asked Dru, coming to Leery's side, her gaze crawling over him, looking for damage, for injuries.

"I don't know," said Ice. "They just went off on your partner."

Atekhomen stepped into the shelter of the trees, a mourning wailing wind rising and rushing past him to blow the gnomes hither and yon. "Now, Summoner?" he cried. "These are ripe for the kill."

"Gather as many as you can," said Ice. "We need to arrest them, so only hurt the ones who resist."

"Joy of joys," said Atekhomen in a voice as flat and dead as the void. "Come on, little ones," he chimed. "Gather around so I may capture you."

"You see, Arvidar?" shouted Jenkor from farther down the path. "They attack us!" He stood pointing at them, about fifty identically dressed gnomes coming down the path behind him.

"But they're cops," said the gnome wearing the biggest crimson hat.

"But they attack us in our own circle!" cried Jenkor. "And we *pay* to be left alone."

Dru began crafting rune sets with both hands, and Leery hunched, his hackles rising, a low growl issuing from deep in his chest. "Uh, we'd better get backup," said Dru.

Ice shrugged. "Yeah." He snapped his fingers. "Atekhomen! Bring those you have and defend us."

"Oh, certainly, Summoner. I had nothing better to do. I enjoy standing around *not* hurting things."

"Just do it!" Ice snapped, pulling out his cell phone and dialing Dawn's number.

"No need to get testy." The eidolon moved out of the trees, multi-hued energy wavering around him, and several gnomes floated in that rainbow-colored sparkle.

"Who are you?" demanded Arvidar. "Why do you pester us? We pay on time!"

"We're the police. We came for information, and some of your gang attacked my partner. Stand down, Arvidar, before things get uglier than they already are."

Ice hung up the phone, and sirens started up in the distance. "It's going to be a minute," he whispered.

Arvidar grinned, a malicious gleam in his eye. "Bet you just found out your backup is a ways off. Bet your friend just found out you're on your own for ten, maybe fifteen minutes."

Dru shook her head.

Arvidar pointed at her and laughed. "I can see it in your face. That's why we *pay* them, you know."

"Okay," said Dru. "But you're going to go first."

"Go?" Arvidar spread his hands and looked around in mock confusion. "Where is it you think I'm going?"

Dru laughed, and overhead grim black clouds rolled in from the horizon. "You don't know me, gnome." She flicked her fingers and lightning danced from the bruised clouds to the ground. A moment later thunder boomed, seeming to shake the trees in the wooded park. "I am Drusilla bat Agrat bat Mahlat, Princess of Gehenna, Heir to the Black and Red Throne, Daughter of the Sovereign of Demons, of the Commander of the Eighteen Legions, of the Queen of Shabbat, She of the Great and Terrible Name." As she spoke, her voice deepened, roughened. "My uncle is Lucifer, the King of Gehenna, King of the Bottomless Pit, Apollyon, Ruler of Demons, Son of Perdition, the Fallen Star, the Father of Lies, Leviathan, and Ruler of Darkness." Her aspect grew frightful, her eyes seeming to glow in the gathering gloom. "If you think *I* need backup, then step forward." Her feet lifted off the ground, and a horrible-smelling wind swirled through the park, bringing the scents of burnt flesh, sulfur, and decay with it. Power crackled from her fingertips like static electricity, and glowing ball lightning danced around her head.

Atekhomen turned toward her with an awe-filled expression. "Oh, Summoner!" he cried. "Forgive me for doubting you! This is the most fun I've had in...*eons*!"

"Glad I could help," whispered Ice.

"Well?" demanded Dru, her voice rolling like thunder between the high-rises of Stuyvesant Town.

Arvidar glanced at Jenkor, then at Reknad, arching his eyebrows.

Leery took a menacing step forward, snarling like a mad dog, drool draping from his bottom lip in long strands.

"Get ready," said Ice. "If they attack, do what you must to protect the three of us."

Atekhomen turned toward him, wearing a smile of pure glee. "What a grand day! I'll be happy to add my power to *hers*, but if you think she needs my help, you've got a few screws loose." He turned and moved to stand next to Dru. "My Lady Chaos," he murmured and inclined his head when she glanced at him.

Arvidar turned slowly, his gaze crawling over his troops, counting, assessing. His gaze narrowed at the expressions of fear and tightened at the expressions of judgment on some faces. He shot a glare at Jenkor. "You got us into this. You lead the charge."

Jenkor swallowed hard but nodded. He moved to take Arvidar's place in the vanguard, but the gnome pushed him toward the policemen, then snapped his gaze at Reknad. "You too, Machete!" He swept his hands forward. "Hit them from two sides!"

Leery threw his head back and howled, turning toward the gnomes who'd escaped Atekhomen's rainbow.

"Show us what you two have got," sneered Arvidar. "Since you think you can make decisions without consulting me!"

Leery grinned his wolfish grin. *Smart,* he thought. *Avoid a potential loss while making his biggest rivals look incompetent.*

Jenkor winced as his gaze flicked from gnome to gnome. "Come, gnomes!" he cried. "We can take them!" He turned toward Reknad and nodded.

The Machete glanced at the reduced number of gnomes around him, then at Atekhomen and the seemingly sleeping gnomes that still bobbed around him. He raised his glance to Leery's face and sneered.

Leery took another menacing step toward them, and Reknad dropped his gaze and seemed to deflate a little.

"Don't give in to fear!" cried Jenkor. "We have the numbers!"

"But they're so big," shouted a gnome hidden in the back of the pack.

"Size means *nothing!*" roared Jenkor. "It's numbers that matter! Come on!" He turned and glared at the cops, then started walking toward them, his fists clenched at his side. When he didn't hear the tromp of marching feet behind him, he faltered, then turned to look over his shoulder.

Arvidar leered at him, a knowing twinkle in his eyes. "They won't follow you, Rake. *They* know that Arvidar the Reaper is the only Gardener who can ensure their continued dominance. That I'm the only gnome for the job!"

Jenkor's shoulders slumped, and he dropped his gaze to the ground.

Arvidar met Dru's eyes. "You can take them, those that you've already captured. Plus, you can take my so-called captains, since they think they know better than me what to do. Let them solve their own problems." He lifted a hand and snapped his fingers. "But don't come back here. Don't ever come back."

The gnomes behind him began to back off the concrete path, and, when their bare feet touched earth, they sank into it as though it were water. The gnomes who'd supported Reknad faded into the earth beneath them. At last, the only gnomes still present were the ones Atekhomen kept in stasis, Reknad, Jenkor, and Arvidar.

The Reaper glanced at the bushes to either side of the path. "Jenkor will answer your questions," he said quietly. "He knows the drill."

Dru settled back to the concrete path. "Okay," she said simply.

"Next time, come with respect," said Arvidar. "Or at least the appearance of it. I have a reputation to uphold."

"Sure. We get it," said Ice.

"We still make curdles, but I don't think your dead angel got it from us," said Arvidar. "Check the Leprechauns. We've had words lately."

"But I thought they cut with Lucky Charms," said Dru.

"They do, but they know what everyone else cuts with, too. Plus, they ain't above buying our product and lacing it with an overdose of ground Cheez-Its or Cheeto powder, then reselling it."

"Why?" grated Leery as he changed back. "Why would they do that?"

"Make us look bad." Arvidar shrugged. "Plus, we've had words about things. And we're growing, while they are shrinking."

"You going to war with them?" asked Ice.

Arvidar turned a shrewd gaze on him. "I remember you."

"Ice Cofy."

"Yeah, I know. You were always smarter than the rest. You let me worry over who's going to war." He nodded at Jenkor. "Jenkor knows everything. He'll talk to you if he knows what's good for him."

4

Leery looped his spare tie around his neck and tied it with efficient flicks of his fingers. He watched as Cofy got the gnomes loaded into a paddy wagon, his gaze straying from time to time to the eidolon, who stood grinning at everyone and everything.

"What kicked it off?" asked Dru in a quiet voice.

"Ice and me, we sort of had a bet." Leery shrugged. "Maybe I came on too strong."

"A bet?"

"Yeah, whoever could get information the quickest got to drive."

"What if I won?"

"Uh... We didn't consider that."

"Uh-huh," she said with a laugh in her voice.

"What was all that about?" Leery asked. "All the pyrotechnics and floating and booming voice and all."

Dru chuckled. "It worked, didn't it? Everyone's going to know soon, anyway. I might as well use it to my advantage when there's a need."

"Sure," said Leery with a shrug. "Why not?"

"Come on," she said, straightening his collar.

"You buy it? What Arvidar said about the Leprechauns?"

Dru shrugged. "It's worth checking out. But in the meantime, we've got Jenkor and Reknad to question."

5

Leery walked into the interview room with two mugs of coffee and glanced at Dru, who sat showing her profile to the gnome seated across from her. She examined her nails and tsked. "Daddy's home. Now you're in for it, Reknad," she said.

Without so much as pausing, Leery kicked the chair out from under the gnome and set Dru's mug down on the table, then took a large swig from his own. "Is *little* Reknad playing hard to get?"

"He's being quite rude," said Dru.

"Reknad!" scolded Leery. "What did I say before I left?"

Reknad climbed to his feet, rubbing his backside. "Screw you, copper."

"Don't you gnomes get cable?" Leery grunted. He walked around the table and sat next to Dru. "No one says copper anymore. It's pig or asshole. You sound like you're trapped in a Sam Spade movie."

Reknad righted his chair and climbed up into it. "I'm telling my magister about this. Police brutality," he said with a nod.

Leery raised an eyebrow at Dru. "He asked for a magister?"

"Not a word," said Dru. "You remember I read you your rights, Reknad? You remember you can have a magister any time you ask for one, and we have to stop the interview until he arrives."

"Yeah, yeah," said the gnome with a flap of his hand. "I don't want one." He scoffed. "I can't have one until this is over. Arvidar said so."

"If it's the cost, we can get you one at no charge."

"Nuh-unh."

Leery turned toward the mirrored glass and arched his eyebrow. Someone tapped the glass twice from the other side. "Okay, then. Just remember, Reknad. All you have to do is ask."

"Right, right, but like I said, I don't want one. Arvidar said to help you, and that's what I have to do, no matter how much I *hate* you."

"Oh, now I'm hurt," said Leery. "We know the Gardeners are still making curdles. We know you are still selling it, and that you've had recent trouble with the Little Gray Men and the Leprechauns."

Reknad scoffed. "Those Irish bastards are jealous." He cackled like a madman. "They invented the stuff, yet the Curdled-brains come see us more often than not. And it's *not* because the Leprechauns are uptown. It's because our product is better. Everyone says so."

Leery nodded and thumped a picture of Raguel on the table, her nostrils caked with orange powder. The forensic photographer had managed to capture some of her holy smoke as she began to disintegrate. "Did Raguel say so? Before she overdosed and *died*?"

"How should I know? I've never seen her in my life."

"Didn't you tell me she looked familiar? Back in Stuyvesant Town?"

"No," said the gnome, shaking his head. "I said I never seen her. And I haven't."

"Tell me your secret ingredient," said Dru.

Reknad sneered. "I thought you knew everything. If you don't even know the ingredient, that means you've got nothing at all linking the Gardeners to the winger."

"Mozzarella from the pizza shop," said Dru.

Reknad tried for a grimace, but he ended up with a scared, guilty expression. "Nuh-unh."

"Yuh-hunh," said Leery. "Selling a few snacks is one thing—I mean, what's the harm?" Leery shook his head. "But killing an angel... That's got ramifications in this life and the next."

"Told you!" snapped Reknad. "The Gardeners didn't kill no angel. We didn't make no hot batch and sell it to Curdled-brains, no matter how worthless they all are."

"You sure about all that?" asked Dru.

"Yeah, you don't seem to like your customers much."

"What's to like? I see them all day, every day. Begging, whining for a taste. It's disgusting."

"And yet you keep on selling to them, don't you?"

Reknad shrugged. "There's money to be made."

Leery slurped his coffee and shook his head. "Why'd Arvidar want us to collar you?"

"Because we screwed up, Jenkor and me."

"Then why not discipline you in-house?"

Reknad shook his head. "That's Gardener business."

"I don't know, Dru," said Leery, turning away from Reknad. "It seems to me that sending his captains in to us might seem like what an innocent gnome would do. At least to Arvidar."

"Ha!" said Reknad. "You're too stupid to be a cop."

"I think he wanted these two out of the way. On ice," said Dru in a dreamy tone. "So he could make whatever deals he wanted without someone in the gang challenging his ideas."

Reknad laughed. "You two should take this show on the road."

Leery sighed. "Fine. Tell us about the Leprechauns. Tell us who we should be looking at."

The gnome narrowed his eyes and nodded. "Eamon Mac Gille Chomhghaill and Luchaidh Ó Laoghaire do their cooking. Start there."

"Cooks?" Leery lifted an eyebrow. "Like we can just go uptown and ask around for the Leprechauns' main cooks. Get real, Reknad. Who gives the orders? Who makes the strategy? Who would want to weed the Gardeners out?"

Reknad shrugged. "Beircheart Mac Ailin. Or maybe Muircheartach Mac Cárthaigh."

Leery opened his mouth to speak but Van Helsing stuck her head through the glass and cleared her throat. "Detectives," she said and beckoned them.

6

Van Helsing led them into the squad room and waved to Ice Cofy. "He chatted up one of the low-level gnomes as he ran him through the system. The gnome came up with some spontaneous utterances and asked to speak to the LM's office."

As Ice approached, Leery arched his eyebrows. "Do I have to ride in the back?"

"Damn right you do," said Ice with a grin. "Listen, Arvidar set all this up. He—"

"According to the gnome you spoke with."

"Well, *duh*. Arvidar knew we'd come around to the Gardeners eventually. He stationed Jenkor and Reknad to wait for us. He told them to volunteer some information implicating the Leprechauns, and if that didn't look viable, to force a confrontation. This whole thing ran according to his plan, including giving us both of his top lieutenants to grill. He's promised them the best magisters if any charges are leveled against them but also said to play along, to tell us what we want to hear."

"All the while steering us toward the Leprechauns."

"Right. My guy says the Leprechauns have nothing to do with this. He said Arvidar had Reknad buy some curdles from them and re-cut it with mozzarella three days ago."

"And maybe that blurred the analysis Hendrix did," added Van Helsing.

"He made them memorize four names: Eamon Mac Gille Chomhghaill, Luchaidh Ó

Laoghaire, Muircheartach Mac Cárthaigh, and—"

"Beircheart Mac Ailin. Reknad just spilled all four names," said Dru.

"Along with a plausible reason why the Leprechauns would want to set up the Gardeners."

"All to lay a foundation of doubt," said Van Helsing. "This Arvidar's a jigsy cove."

Ice arched his eyebrows, but Leery shook his head.

"Right, Lieu," said Dru. "So, what do we do? Play along? Go see the Leprechauns?"

"Hmm," murmured Van Helsing.

At that moment, Ice's cell phone jangled inside his pocket, and he fished it out. "Cofy," he said. He glanced up at Leery and held up his index finger. "How long ago?" he asked. "Right. We'll be right over." He hung up the phone and grimaced. "This just got more complicated," he said.

"Tell us," said Dru.

"Dawn just took a report of numinous fire in Tompkins Square Park."

"Let me guess," said Leery. "The Little Gray Men just got hit."

"Get over there," said Van Helsing in a grim tone. "Get over there and put a stop to this before it turns into a weirding war."

"You got it, Lieu," said Leery, already heading toward the elevators.

7

Dawn Bogue leaned against the SWAT C3 tractor-trailer a block and a half from Tompkins Square Park, glaring down at her nails. She grimaced as Leery screeched to a stop, and he, Dru, and Ice jumped out. "The servitors are locking down the park and sweeping it," she said. "It's pretty ugly in there."

"Big G?" asked Dru.

Dawn shook her head. "Most of the Little Gray Men got hit. Most are already dead, and the ones that aren't wish they were." She sighed. "We won't get anything from them for weeks, even if they survive." She waved her hand at the park. "And we won't get in there for hours with these SWAT geeks in charge."

"And we're sure about the magic?" asked Leery. "Numinous?"

Dawn nodded once. "According to the eyewitnesses, the descriptions of the attack match."

"So, we either have an act of revenge for the death of Raguel, or..." said Dru.

"Or those witnesses are card-carrying members of the Gardeners," finished Leery.

Dawn swept a narrowed-eyed gaze from Ice's face to Dru's and then to Leery's. "Tell me."

"We may have uncovered a little plot," said Ice with a sweeping wave toward the north and Stuyvesant Town.

"Seems Arvidar is directing a play for our entertainment," said Leery with a grimace. "He doesn't know I prefer musicals."

Cofy arched an eyebrow at him, then turned back to Dawn. "He gave us some of his crew to interrogate—either because he wants us to know the information but can't appear to help us willingly or for more nefarious reasons," said Ice.

"Like wanting to get rid of several sets of enemies with our help." Leery sucked his teeth.

"This numinous fire..." Dru shook her head. "It's a little obvious, no?"

"Well...yeah," said Leery. "Then again, ever hear of Sodom and Gomorrah? Angels aren't exactly known for their subtlety, either."

"No, they aren't," agreed Dru. "But still, if this attack is a red herring...if anyone other than the Angel of Wrath—"

"Or maybe an Angel of Judgment," said Ice.

"—perpetrated this attack, then it would have to be someone who could either create the conditions in which they could manifest angelfire, or—"

"Manipulate the perceptions of the witnesses so that they *saw* angelfire where some other magic manifested," said Dawn. She stared at Dru. "Reality warp?"

"Could be," said Dru. "Could very easily be that."

"You mean, the Leprechauns might have done this?" asked Leery.

"It's possible," said Dawn.

"Naw," said Ice. "I know some of them. This isn't their style."

"Their *style*?" scoffed Leery.

"Yeah, man, their style. The Leprechauns I know from way back when I worked edibles are a physical bunch. Super strength, super speed, telekinetic, shapeshifters. Those are things I'd expect from a Leprechaun attack."

"Yeah," said Dawn with a sigh. "This is..."

"More cunning," said Dru. "Or it really was Samael or some other holy roller."

Leery shrugged. "Or one of the Nephilim."

"One way to find out," said Ice, arching his eyebrows at Dawn.

"Yeah, I can reach out to Puriel."

"You know Puriel?" asked Leery.

"Yeah," she said. "I used to date Tezcatlipoca, and they knew one another. Close friends, actually."

"Tezcatlipoca? How did the Smoking Mirror become friends with the Fiery One?" asked Dru.

Dawn shrugged. "I asked Tezy that once. He only laughed and said, 'Where there's smoke, there's fire.'" She shrugged, then pushed away from the C3. "Come on, I'll introduce you."

"Great," grunted Dru.

Leery glanced at her. "Problems?"

"He's an asshole," said Dru. "So judgmental!"

"You've met him?"

Dawn pursed her lips. "He always seemed nice to me."

"He is, and I quote, fiery and pitiless. He doesn't treat my kind very well."

"Well, he can deal with me if he wants to act like a thug," said Leery.

"I'm sure he'll be the perfect gentleman," said Dawn with a worried frown. "Tezy is also known as Titlacauan." When everyone looked at her blankly, she dropped her gaze. "It means 'we are his slaves,' and it just illustrates how worshippers sometimes make their gods like men—equipped with both light and dark sides."

"I hope you're right," said Dru. "I'm just not super comfortable in the presence of Angels of Judgment."

Leery rested a hand on her shoulder, and she grinned up at him.

"Come on," said Dawn. "We can zip over there in the hours it will take the servitors to finish processing over the park."

"Zip over there?" asked Leery.

"Yeah, Puriel lives in the Palisades."

"The Palisades…"

"Sure. Tezy has a house there, too."

8

Dawn drove down the tree-lined and aptly named Forest Lane, passing one giant estate after another. Each was tucked into its own copse of trees, which was, in turn, encapsulated in a larger wood.

"It's too bad angels have to live like paupers," Leery said with a sarcastic twang. "So much for vows of poverty making you more holy."

Dawn glanced at him in the mirror and smiled. "You ain't seen nothing yet. These are the small estates—and none of them are owned by angels."

"Small..." Leery glanced out the window and scoffed. "After we're done, we can run by the Upper West Side. I'll show you my place."

They followed the road until it dead-ended in a massive compound that overlooked the Hudson. Dawn pulled the car around the square median and parked in front of the main walk. "Here we are," she said as she opened the door and got out. "Come on." She led them to the thick double doors and rang the bell.

"You sure he's here?" asked Ice.

"Most likely," said Dawn with a shrug. "He's almost always here."

"So he certainly could have zipped over to Tompkins Square," said Leery as he glanced down at his watch.

"And why would I do that?" asked a rich baritone voice from the other side of the door. Locks clicked, and the door opened to reveal an ordinary-looking man—if you ignored the waxy white wings—tall and thin, wispy white-blond hair swept to the side, and wire-framed glasses pushed up on his forehead. "Dawn!" he exclaimed, and his eyes glowed golden as he stepped forward to wrap her in a hug.

"Hello, Puriel," she said.

While he hugged her, Puriel's gaze probed the others, with a slight narrowing of his eyes when he looked at Dru. "Fellow police officers," he murmured. "My, my."

"I'm afraid it isn't a social call, Puriel," said Dawn.

"No, I'd expect not," he said, staring at Dru. "Well, come on. The air is best on the rear patio this time of year." He turned and led them through the massive house and out a set of French doors that opened on a concrete patio. He took the seat at the round table that would afford him the best view of the Hudson and held his hands out to either side. "Sit. Can I offer you anything?"

"Would coffee be too much trouble?" asked Leery

Puriel smiled. "Of course not, Detective Oriscoe." His smile widened at Leery's look of surprise and confusion. "Oh, you have no secrets from me, Detective." He turned his gaze toward Dru, and his face lost several degrees of warmth. "No one does."

"Hmm," said Leery. "The last guy who said that to me lives in Gehenna."

Puriel's face darkened a little. "*He* and I do not speak any longer. I try to surround myself with like-minded individuals."

"Must make for a boring life."

Smiling a lopsided smile, Puriel shrugged. "At times. But I do have friends who aren't angels. Tezy, for instance." He nodded at Dawn. "And Dawn."

A woman in a French maid's get-up delivered a tray of coffee and Puriel waved them to it. He glanced at Dawn and tilted his head to the side. "Numinous fire? In Alphabet City? And for *revenge*?" He tsked and shook his head. "Hardly. If He instructed me to, I would loose angelfire on the City in a moment, but *only* if He told me to."

"Eyewitnesses said otherwise," said Leery sipping his coffee. His eyes widened. "Hey! This is better than Starbucks!"

"It's the holy water," said Puriel with pleasure twinkling in his eyes. "I'm delighted you find it tasty. But back to your witnesses, they must be mistaken." A small smile played at the corners of his mouth. "If they even exist."

Leery grinned. "I meant about the angelfire, not that you—"

"Perhaps one of the Nephilim?" asked Dru.

Puriel scoffed. "They, too, know better. The Lord of Heaven brooks no disobedience to his laws." His eyes seemed to bore into hers.

"What if they were being attacked?" She met his gaze head-on and didn't flinch.

"Self-defense isn't a plausible reason to employ numinous fire. It's reserved for the Lord's will. Besides, a martyred Nephilim would see certain…benefits…certain *advantages* in the Kingdom of Heaven. They have more motivation not to employ such…uh…nuclear measures."

"I see." Dru sat back in her chair, looking at her hands.

"Things are more…*lawful* in my home realm, uh, Your Grace."

"Must make for a boring life," repeated Leery with a grin.

Puriel laughed, loud and boisterous, his baritone guffaws reaching out toward the Hudson and echoing back. "I only wish, Detective," he said as his laughter died down to a chuckle. "Many believe that certain angels fell and that was the end of it. As you no doubt know from your...*work*, temptation is a constant threat. No, there are always those tempted by the things they see in this realm—or in Gehenna."

"Like Raguel?" asked Leery.

"Alas, poor Raguel. Yes, Detective. She has fallen and has paid the price. Poetic justice, perhaps."

"Are you sure you didn't have something to do with that?" asked Ice.

"Yes, Detective Cofy. I'm quite sure. I don't deal with such banalities as overdoses. When I come, I come bearing the might of the Lord of Hosts in my hand and Yahweh's wrath beneath my wings. I come in the shining light of righteousness, not the shadows of an alley in Tribeca."

"And how did you know where she perished?" asked Dru.

"I know where all of the Host are at any given moment."

"Even in this realm?"

"In *any* realm," said Puriel. "It's necessary for my responsibilities."

Dru lifted her chin and let it drop.

"Say, could I trouble you for a refill?" asked Leery, looking mournfully into his empty coffee cup.

"Of course, Detective." Puriel lifted a languid hand and snapped his fingers, though no one stood on the patio to hear it. "I'll have a thermos made up for you as well."

"Mighty decent of you."

Puriel waved that away. "Back to your issues in Tompkins Square," he said in a grave voice. "I fear you are dealing with an imposter. None of the Host were in that part of town—"

"But what about—" began Dru.

"—and none of the Nephilim, either. I doubt the actual spell used will bear the signatures of angelfire. I'd be happy to assist your ME in the analysis. Will it be Liz Hendrix? I do love working with her."

"Uh..." said Leery. "How do you know Liz?"

Puriel showed him a small grin. "A gentleman never speaks of such things."

"Oh...well...yeah, I'm sure it will end up with Liz. At the moment, the SWAT team has the scene."

Puriel arched an eyebrow. "Shall we go assist them?"

Leery glanced at Dru then Ice, then shrugged. "Sure, why not?"

Puriel lifted his hand once more and snapped. A brilliant light strobed around them momentarily, and when it faded, they stood on the corner of 7th Street and Avenue B. Puriel turned toward the park and squinted his eyes.

"Um, what about our car?" asked Dawn.

"And that coffee?" asked Leery hopefully.

Puriel's hand came up and yet another snap sounded. The cruiser rocked on its shocks at the curb, and the same woman in the French maid's outfit stood blinking at the sun. She held a large ceramic mug in one hand and a giant YETI thermos in the other.

"Ah," said Leery. "Thanks."

Without another word, Puriel strode down the tree-lined cement path toward the center of Tompkins Square Park, leaving the NYPD detectives to follow.

A glowing servitor rocketed toward them, moving as fast as lightning, though as silent as the plague. "Hey! This is a crime scene! You can't—"

Puriel waved a hand as if brushing away a fly, and the servitor disintegrated in a puff of sun-bright particles.

"Uh…" said Leery. "That might not be the best way to—"

With a grinding crash, three servitors appeared out of thin air, arrayed in a semi-circle before them. "Halt! We are servitor warriors with the—"

Puriel waved his hand again, and again, the servitors burst apart, the motes that remained fading away like embers from spent fireworks.

"—deal with the…" Leery let his words fade away, shaking his head. "Maybe we could talk to them a second before you banish them? Think you could work that into your plan?"

Puriel glanced at him, eyes glowing. "Command them to stop casting their feeble spells at me, then."

"Well, if you'll let us *talk* to them…"

"Ah. My apologies." Puriel turned away, then stepped off the path and moved toward the playground. "The attack happened over here…"

"Dawn, can you—"

"Already on it," she said, phone to her ear.

"Yes, a powerful spell," muttered Puriel. "But *not* angelfire. No, this was meant to leave a residue *like* angelfire, but this was a..." He stopped and narrowed his eyes, snapping his head toward the center of the park once more. "Who could be so stupid?" He turned and moved toward the Krishna Tree. "The idiot is still here!"

"Wait a minute, Puriel!" said Ice. "How about letting us in on the joke?"

Puriel lifted his hand and pointed at the venerable American Elm standing near the center of the park. "A *presence* lingers in that tree! He watches us, even now!"

"Uh, what kind of presence?" asked Leery, handing his thermos and mug to Dru and loosening his tie. She looked at him a moment, then squatted and set them on the sidewalk.

"An old one. A member of the Seelie Court." Puriel stormed toward the tree, a brilliant gold-white fire shimmering into existence and settling around his shoulders like a cloak. His wings flapped, battling the sun for the brightest thing visible. "Woe to those who call evil good and good evil, who put darkness for light and light for darkness, who put bitter for sweet and sweet for bitter!" His voice thundered across the park, setting off car alarms for blocks in all directions. "Beware, evildoer! For those who plow evil and those who sow trouble reap it!" He raised his arm, pointing at the tree. "Reveal yourself, for the Lord of Hosts already sees you!"

"Oh, goodie," murmured Leery. "A sermon."

Puriel grunted a word in Enochian, a word that sounded like a loving caress and yet made Leery wince. A bolt of pure gold lightning streaked from his fingertip with an air-rending crackle and tickled the air near the tree—but there was nothing there.

And yet, a harsh cry sounded. "Ach! Piss off ye great winged dosser!" The voice coming from nowhere bordered on a woman's contralto.

"Show yourself, worm!" thundered Puriel.

"Feck off, ye gammy dove!"

"Oh, no," said Dru quietly. "Another slang slinger."

"In the name of the Most High, I command thee, worm! Show yourself!"

"And I says, feck off, ye Holy Joe! I don't answer to the likes of ye!"

Puriel extended his finger and another golden lightning bolt arced toward another empty spot of air, this time several paces from the tree.

"Oh, ye manky moran! Ye feckless feckwit! Ye thick culchie!"

Puriel shot his finger forward a third time, and a thick band of gold arced away toward yet a third location. When it struck, thunder rolled in the sky. "Do as I say!"

"You want I should shew meself, do ye? Be careful what ye ask for ye great feckin' eejit!" The wrenching squeal of tearing metal accompanied the last syllable, and a park bench ripped away from its concrete slab and blurred toward Puriel, but the angel only waved his hand and the bench slammed into the earth fifteen feet short. At the same moment, the air where the lightning had struck last shimmered into a screen of light fog. "Well, here I am, boyo! Right here, standin' in the bright sun for all to see!" A dark shadow moved behind the mist, something that twisted and hunched and grew.

"Uh, Puriel?" asked Leery, pulling his shirt and coat off over his head and holding them out to Dru, who only cocked her head and narrowed her eyes at him. She took them but let them drop to the grass.

"What is it, Detective?"

"*Show meself I will!*" The mist burned away in a flash of bright white light, revealing a hulking creature of bunched muscles covered in rough-looking dusky skin. Red hair capped the lumpy skull, and his eyes flashed and shone with bright emerald green power. His hands ended in thick, blunt fingers about as thick as a soda can. The Hyde-like beastman flexed his hands into fists and shook them at Puriel. "Well? Are ye delira and excira, ye earwiggin' pigeon? Ye gawkin' bat?"

"Oh, boy," said Leery, and Dru began spinning crimson runes in the air.

Behind him, Cofy chanted, "*Haere mai ki ahau,* Atekhomen! *Ae, haere mai, he kaha. Haere mai ki taku awhina, tohea to mana!*"

With a grunting bark, Dawn dropped her phone as her skin began to flow and change, melding with her clothing, becoming thick black fur. Her bones crackled and popped beneath her skin, morphing into the skeleton of a great cat. At the same time, she hunched forward on all fours and roared, lifting her snout to the sky, even as her teeth reformed, becoming massive fangs.

"Show off," growled Leery, his voice gravelly with his own change. She flicked a disdainful glance his way, then padded into the trees beside the path.

"Sssss-summoner," hissed Atekhomen as the golden light of his summoning swelled and dimmed.

"Will ye look at this holy show?" grumbled the leprechaun in his now-basso voice. "Ye brought your friends and I's just by me lonesome. Where's yer fairness? Where's yer *righteousness*?" He spat the last word as if it tasted bad.

"Step forward, worm, and taste my righteousness," said Puriel in an almost-bored voice.

"Oh, *aye*," said the beastman. "Watch therefore; for ye know not what hour your death doth come."

"*Blasphemer!*" Puriel shouted in his gong-like voice. He pointed at the leprechaun and yet another golden bolt danced from his fingertip, but this time, it tore right through the creature and split a tree behind him.

"Howya, Holy Joe," said the basso voice, but this time from right beside them. A massive fist arced out of thin air and slammed into the side of Puriel's head, knocking him to the ground.

"Oh! How fun!" shouted Atekhomen in his molten copper voice. "Shall I kill it, Summoner? Or shall I kill the Winged One?"

"No killing! Subdue the leprechaun!"

"Oh, no, boyo!" shouted the leprechaun. "Kill it! Kill us both, if you can!" He booted Puriel in the side, sending the angel skittering across the ground toward the massive elm tree near the center of the park. Then, he whirled and beckoned to the eidolon. "Come, ye hunk of stink!"

With a snarl, Leery leaped, fangs stretched wide, head angled to lay his jaws along the leprechaun's neck. At the same moment, Dawn burst from the brush behind the beastman, a black blur, moving as silently as death.

"Feck off, cull!" the leprechaun grunted, swatting Leery away as if he presented no more threat than an irksome gnat.

Dru muttered a harsh phrase in the *Verba Patiendi* and hurled a scarlet eleven-pointed rune set at him, already spinning blue runes with her left hand, her gaze on Leery.

The moment Dawn pounced on the leprechaun's back, Atekhomen struck, swinging both anvil-like fists, one high, one low. The Mr. Hyde version of the leprechaun began a harsh peel of laughter, but then Dawn landed on his back, sharp sable claws gouging into his thick rough skin. Her head darted forward and clamped on the back of his neck, long fangs driving deep toward his arteries. The leprechaun's laughter choked off into a squeal, and he took two staggering steps forward—right into Atekhomen's on-coming fists.

"*Whakamatihia o waewae!*" shouted Ice, pointing at the leprechaun's hairy flat feet. A chunk of Atekhomen dropped off the back of the eidolon and snaked, as quick as lightning, to the beastman's feet, wrapping around them, then digging into the concrete beneath them.

Dru connected seven azure runes with golden lines and hurled the set at Leery's crumpled form, barking a phrase in the spidery language she sometimes used. The runes grew brighter and brighter as they flew, spinning at him, and as they settled across his hunched back, they burned white-bright. Leery arched his back and hissed, and Dru turned back toward the leprechaun, drawing acid-yellow figures in the air before her.

The leprechaun tried to whirl, tried to throw Dawn from his back, and as he did, a horrendous crack sounded, and the concrete beneath his feet shattered. He took two clunky steps, peering down at the copper binding on his feet. Atekhomen smashed one fist into his forehead, driving the leprechaun back one stumbling step, and then the beastman roared in anger, put his head down, and charged right at the eidolon, crook-fingered hands flung toward Atekhomen's neck.

Dawn hissed and arched her back, digging into the leprechaun's back with her claws and clamping her jaws tighter. Leery raced in from the side, bent low, and dove at the beastman's driving legs. Atekhomen side-stepped, threw one fast jab, then two, then three, and the leprechaun staggered away.

"Get his arms!" Ice shouted at Dru, then pointed at the leprechaun's knees. "*Huihui mai, e tika nei!*" The copper blobs around the beastman's feet liquified and flowed up his shins, then extruded wire-like strands toward each other, wrapping around his knees and cinching them tight.

With a squawk, the leprechaun tottered a step, then slid over sideways.

Dru completed her runes and empowered them with a burst of *Verba Patiendi*, then hurled two five-pointed stars of yellow runes at him, but before the creature could crash to the ground, he disappeared with a pop of rushing air, leaving Dawn to flop down on top of the chunks of now-empty copper. Dru's runes slapped into her and bound her front paws together. "Sorry!" she called, working to dispel the rune set.

Atekhomen blurred away toward the elm tree, the air growing hot with his passage, and small bolts of lightning crackling in his wake. Before he'd crossed half the distance to the tree, thunder boomed, and a bolt of lightning as thick as a man's thigh arced from the heavens and slammed into the earth, flinging soil and grass in every direction. A sound like that of an iron-barred jail cell slamming shut rent the air, and Puriel's voice lanced into the sky, *"In His Holy Name, I command you to be still!"*

A silence fell over the park in the wake of his command, then Puriel picked himself up from the ground and dusted himself off. He glanced toward the detectives and beckoned them. "Come, my friends. I've restrained the lout."

Atekhomen paused, glancing over his shoulder at Ice. Dawn loped toward Puriel, moving like a thundercloud's shadow across the grass. With a grunt, Leery went toward his belongings and transformed.

"Dru! You just dumped my clothes all in a heap!"

"Oh, did I?" asked Dru in a flat tone as she turned toward him. "Gee, I'm sorry. I thought I was your Warder, not your maid." She whirled and stalked away toward the park's exit.

"What? I..." Leery took a step after her, faltered, then looked down at the pile of clothing.

"Way to go, player," said Ice. "You've got a way with women, don't you?" The detective shrugged and walked toward his eidolon, grinning.

"It's a gift," muttered Leery in a sour tone.

9

The servitors glowered at Puriel as the angel led the leprechaun—now wrapped in massive silver chains the Angel of Judgment had snapped into existence—out of the park. The detectives followed the pair, with Leery bringing up the rear, looking glum, the mug of coffee in one hand, the thermos in the other.

"We will take custody of the prisoner," said one of the servitors in a clanging voice.

"No, you shall not," said Puriel in melodious and mild tones.

"We've got this," Ice said. "We need to interview him at the Two-Seven. You are welcome to observe."

"Are you kidding me? He just burned half the park!" snapped one of the servitors.

"He might have. We'll ask him about that, too, and you can have him when we're finished. But for now, he's ours."

"We'll just see about that!" snapped the servitor. "We'll call—"

"Call whoever you want, pal," said Leery. "But it's a waste of time. Trust me. We're on the GC's snack task force. On the premiere case, you could say. The Chief of D's will back us up."

The servitor went completely still as if frozen in place.

"I think he just put us on hold," said Leery.

"Come," said Puriel, lifting his hand to snap.

"Uh, why don't we drive? You know, for appearance's sake?"

Puriel arched an eyebrow at him.

"Otherwise, we'll have to schlepp back down here for the cars."

"Ah," said Puriel. He gazed at the cars for a moment and both disappeared. "There. Now, we can go." He snapped his fingers before anyone could speak, and suddenly they were all standing in the squad room of the Supernatural Inquisitors Unit.

"Whose vazey idea was this?" demanded Van Helsing from her office door. "Who's the foozler who decided to teleport into a police station? Into *my* police station, my *squad room*?"

"Lieu, meet Puriel. Puriel, meet our lieutenant, Epatha Van Helsing."

The lieu's hand trembled up to her throat. "Puh-puriel?" she murmured.

"Enchanted," said Puriel with a half-bow. "I believe I knew His Grace, your father."

"Uh…"

"And this, Lieu, is the guy behind the Tompkins Square thing," said Leery. "We're about to question him, and you're about to get a pissy call from the SWAT shift commander. He's going to complain that Puriel stole this leprechaun away before their play date. He's going rant and rave and—" Leery snapped his mouth shut as the phone in Van Helsing's office began to ring.

"Is he booked?" she asked, her face contracting into a pained grimace.

"No, uh…"

"I brought us directly here, Lieutenant," said Puriel in a regal tone. "It was most efficient."

"I see." Epatha flapped a hand at Leery. "Put him in the interview room for now, but no one talks to him before I finish wading through this mire." She turned toward her office, flickering like an old fluorescent bulb.

"I could question him," said Puriel. "After all, I do not work for the NYPD, and technically, both this crime and Raguel's death fall under my jurisdiction."

"No," said Van Helsing. "Please do as I ask."

Puriel twitched his shoulders. "Then I shall wait."

Van Helsing nodded and disappeared. After the space of a breath, she answered her phone and began a low, murmured conversation.

"Come on," said Leery. "Let me show you the interview room."

10

Angie stepped into the observation room, her eyes all but throwing sparks. Her gaze crawled from face to face in the crowded room—from the Chief of D's to Hugo Smith, the Chief of Special Operations, then on to the SWAT shift commander. "Popular room today." She flicked her gaze at Epatha Van Helsing, Ice Cofy, Dawn Bogue, and someone she didn't know—a thin blond-haired man with wire-rimmed glasses and…angel wings. "Chiefs," she said, then nodded to Epatha. "Who stirred up this hornets' nest?"

Still flickering, Epatha hooked her thumb at the thin man. "Meet Puriel," she said. "Puriel, ALM Angie Carmichael."

"Ah," said the angel. "Yes. Ms. Carmichael." His gaze stopped just shy of reaching her eyes.

Angie stopped and cocked an eyebrow at him. "Something wrong, sir?"

"Oh, it's nothing. I keep company with Tezcatlipoca from time to time. I understand the allure of the dark side."

"Sure thing, Obi-Wan. One thing, though. Keep your nose out of my love life."

Puriel treated her to a kindly smile. "I can no more help my nature than your...*friend* can. I don't stick my nose in. I'd have to blind myself to avoid seeing such things."

Angie fought the sneer that wanted to splash across her face and turned to Van Helsing. "I take it he's had his rights read to him?"

"Yes," said the lieu. "And he's signed the waiver with nothing untoward. Everyone in the room saw it and are additional witnesses should it come to it."

Angie sniffed and nodded her head once. "What's his name?" She pointed toward the one-way glass with her chin.

"Muircheartach Mac Cárthaigh."

"Uh...yeah."

Epatha smiled. "Leery dubbed him 'Mack.'"

"Right. Turn it up," she said, nodding toward the intercom.

With a slight grin, Puriel spun the knob.

11

Leery shook his head and slurped the last of Puriel's coffee from the large ceramic mug. He set the mug aside with a mournful sigh, shaking his head a little. "And to think I thought Starbucks could make a cup of coffee."

Dru ignored him, leaning forward on her elbows. "Why'd you do it?" she demanded, her gaze boring into Mack's.

"Ach. Why's yer little woman doin' the talkin'?"

"Careful, pal," said Leery. "She might get offended and try to ruin your clothes."

Dru scoffed. "A 'little woman' too much for you to deal with? I thought the Leprechauns were tough."

"Lassie," Mack said with a sigh, "just 'cause I'm a leprechaun doesn't mean I'm a Leprechaun."

"Are you denying belonging of the gang?" asked Leery, glancing at his empty mug with a frown. "Then why'd you go after the Little Gray Men?"

"Are ye feckin' ossified, man? I've said naught one way or t'other. I just said that bein' a leprechaun doesn't make me part o' th'gang, is all."

"Time for straight answers, Mack," said Leery with a grim frown. "You've signed the waiver. Said you wanted to cooperate."

"Are you in the Leprechaun street gang or aren't you?" asked Dru.

Mack tilted his small head to the side, green eyes twinkling. "Well, now, since ye asked me so nice. Aye, ye could say I'm a leprechaun and a Leprechaun, and you wouldn't be far off t' mark. I only helped *establish* the crew back in the day. It's a matter of honor, lass."

"Is that why you launched the attack on the Little Gray Men? Honor?"

Mack shrugged and pursed his lips. "Ye could say a gnome should keep his lips sealed. Ye could say that telling secrets could get ye in a load o' trouble."

"Retribution, then?" asked Leery. "For what?"

"Oh, ye know, ye fierce mutt." The leprechaun turned his head slightly and treated Leery to an exaggerated wink.

"No, I don't. Why don't you share with the class, Mack?"

A faint smile flickered across Mack's face. "Oh, the games ye do play. But fine. I'll play right along like a good lad." He winked at Dru. "And maybe ye'll give us a wee kiss, lass." As her eyes narrowed, Mack quickly turned back to Leery. "It could be said that sharin' family recipes could lead to some comeuppances, right and true. Could be that I'd hear a leprechaun speak an order to make a hames out of a crew that'd share the Leprechaun's recipes."

"Right, but who exactly said the Little Gray Men leaked your recipes?"

Mack grinned, spreading his lips wide. "Oh, maybe a little bird swooped down from the wide blue and kissed me ear. Or, perhaps a ghost came to us with whispery secrets. Or yet, it could be that one of Hel's own paid us a visit to pay off a debt of honor."

"One of Hel's own?"

"Svartalfar," said Dru. "Black elves."

"Oh," said Leery. "I hate those guys. So snooty."

Dru leaned forward, her gaze drilling into Mack. "And you're admitting, on the record, that you are responsible for the devastation in Tompkins Square Park? That you manifested a reality warp to cover your tracks and make it appear the action of some wayward angel?"

Mack shrugged his tiny shoulders. "Mortified though I am at how it turned out, it seemed like a savage idea at the time. Gave it me best, I did. Me mistake was not legging it, but I wanted to stick around and see it play out. Never expected that dove to come walkin' through." He leaned back in the chair. "Well, now. There ye have it. All the craic, and if it isn't too much to ask, I'd like a room with a plump mattress. I'm shattered."

Dru sat back and glanced at Leery. "Think that's enough for the LM?"

The door swung open, and Angie Carmichael stepped into the room. "You have to testify to all that you just said," she said to Mack.

The leprechaun nodded and looked her up and down. "And maybe *ye'll* give us the wee kiss since this one isn't in a kissy mood?"

Carmichael rolled her eyes. "Lock him up. Drop him into protective custody."

"Lock me up?" Mack's voice cracked up a couple of registers and, for just a moment, his Irish brogue evaporated in favor of a lumpy Brooklyn accent, but then he snapped his mouth shut. When he went on, the brogue was back, heavier than ever, his i's becoming oy's. "Stop acting the maggot! I'll not have some banjaxed jail cell! I expect a grand room in a fine hotel—one with black stuff on tap and room service for miles! And if it's not too much to ask, a view of the skyline would tickle me proper."

"Good luck with that," said Angie. "Dungeons are underground. We've got your confession—but the details are light. Give a full account without all that 'maybe' and 'could be,' and these fine detectives will check it out. If we can make a case out of it, maybe we'll want your testimony and can talk about the motel room." She turned and lay her hand on the doorknob.

Mack sighed and slouched his shoulders. "Fine, fine," he said, dropping his Lucky Charms act and switching back to native New Yorker. "The Svartalfar told us the LGMs snitched us out."

"And which Svartalfar, specifically?" asked Angie, turning back around. Leery stood and offered her his chair, and she sank into it. "And why?"

"They owed us. We helped them settle a little turf dispute on credit. This paid the debt."

"Even if it was a lie?" asked Angie.

"It wasn't," said Mack with a grin.

Angie dropped a yellow legal pad on the table and spun it around toward Mack. She lay a pen down next to it. "Names of the Svartalfar. Names of the Leprechauns who gave you your orders."

"I'll give you the Svartalfar." He picked up the pen and started writing.

"I need the Leprechauns, too."

"And I need a pot of gold so I can retire from the blasted game and move up to the Adirondacks or maybe the Finger Lakes. I need a plush mattress in a fine room way up in the clouds." He waggled his red eyebrows. "And a fine woman such as yourself to share the both of them."

"You can't always get what you need. Sometimes you have to settle for what's on offer," said Angie.

"My point exactly, lass," he said in his rolling stage-Irish.

12

The two chiefs glowered down at Epatha Van Helsing as Leery, Dru, and Angie came out into the squad room. Chief Magnussen towered over her, hunching his shoulders and neck to hear the hissed stream of abuse issuing from the other man—the Chief of Special Operations, dressed as per his habit in a black suit, white shirt, and skinny black tie. Leery grimaced and took a step in their direction, but Van Helsing's flickering gaze met his for a moment and a soft, transient smile warned him off.

"Those damn special ops types are all alike," he muttered.

"Indeed," said Puriel, stepping up behind them. "And in this case, she's taking a chewing for my part in the resolution at Tompkins Square."

"Resolution? *Resolution?*" Leery hissed. "Let me be the first to tell you, pal, ain't nothing resolved."

Puriel arched a thin blond eyebrow at him.

"We started this damn case because that idiot of a Grand Cynosure wants his sound bites. Yeah, your Raguel overdosed, but hey, junkies do that ten times a day in the Locus of New York. What makes her special is that she's the first one since that idiotic 'War on Snacks' speech. So, of course, *we're* ordered onto the case, which takes us to the gnomes and their damn hoes and their damn garden parties. They point us at the Leprechauns and, just like clockwork, we get a rampaging leprechaun hitting a gnome gang in Tompkins Square Park. This is—"

"But surely you can see the linkage. Mack just admitted—"

"Right. *Right*! He just admitted to blowing up the Little Gray Men and pointed us at *yet another group*—this time, the Svartalfar. But the Gardeners' sudden cooperation pointed us at the Leprechauns half a heartbeat before the attack at the park. Don't you see, Puriel? We're like puppets on a string! A leads to B, B points us at C, C tosses the carrot to D. 'Run over here, so we can send you over there in time for you to dance at our command.' That's what Mack's confession is worth!" Leery shook his head. "No. What I want to know is who is behind all this? Who gains from this?"

Dru's light touch on his arm silenced Leery. He'd been near shouting by the end of his rant, and the squad room had gone as quiet as the grave. He twisted his head toward the Chiefs and the lieu and found them staring at him. Van Helsing flickered in and out of phase at a faster rate than before. The Chief of D's gazed at him, flat-eyed but with seeming compassion. Chief Smith, though, glared at him with open hostility over smoked lenses shoved down his nose.

"Oh, don't let us stop you, Detective," Chief Smith said into the silence. "On second thought, do let us stop you. You've screwed this sideways, Oriscoe, like you always do. I'll tell you what, though. I'm willing to wipe the slate clean and give you a fresh start. All I'm asking in return is your cooperation in bringing that Leprechaun to justice. Now, how does that sound?"

"Wow, that sounds like a really good deal, Chief," said Leery with a snarl. "But I think I've got a better one. How about I give you—" Dru's grip tightened on his arm, and he glanced down at her. She shook her head.

"Hugo," said Chief Magnussen. "He's one of mine."

"Just so. He's *one of yours*, and he materially participated in blocking *my men* from doing their jobs, from pursuing the terrorist in the interrogation room." He pulled off his sunglasses and flicked a flesh-colored earpiece from his left ear. "I'm going to be honest with you, Magnussen. I hate this place. I hate this precinct house, this zoo, this locus, this...this...whatever you want to call it. I can't stand it, Magnussen, this slipshod, seat-of-the-pants way of policing supernaturals. I just can't stand it anymore. It's the smell, the gritty shit beneath my shoes, the very air itself. I feel saturated by it. I can taste it every waking moment, and I'm scared by that. I fear it's infected me. It's repulsive. It's...it's..." He held his hands up, rubbing his fingertips together. "I must get out of here. I've got to get back to 1PP where there's some semblance of order at least. Back to a place where things make sense, where rules are followed, lines are *not* crossed at will, and where people *do their fucking jobs*." He turned away from Leery, sliding his sunglass back into place and pushing an earpiece back into his ear. "Every cop on this planet instinctively develops an equilibrium with his fellows, Magnussen, his environment. He knows where the lines are and respects the boundaries. All except *detectives*." He nearly spat the last word. "No, detectives spread out, look over fences, stick their noses in. Their attitudes, their *disrespect* for their superiors, for those natural boundaries…well, it *spreads and spreads and spreads*, like a disease, a plague…like a virus." Smith scoffed and glared up at the Chief of D's. "These *are* your people, Magnussen. I trust you will put your house back in order. Because if you don't, I'm going to the commissioner *and* the mayor—to Cynosure Endymion if I have to!"

Magnussen nodded. "Maybe it is best that you go back to 1PP, Hugo. I'll—"

Chief Smith pushed past him, heading for the squad room's side door. As he did, he turned and glanced at Leery, then tsked. "You hear that, Mr. Oriscoe? That's the sound of inevitability. That's the sound of your career flushing down kismet's tubes. Goodbye, Mr. Oriscoe."

"Hey, it's been real fun. Come back anytime, Chief Smith."

Chief Magnussen shook his head and sighed. "Just once, Oriscoe."

"What's that, Chief?"

"Just once, I'd like you to try to *not* make something worse than it already is." He turned back to Van Helsing. "Get this wrapped up,

Epatha. I'll hold Smith off, but you need to give me ammunition to do it. I need results."

"Yes, Chief," she said. As the giant turned and ducked out into the hall, she hooked her finger at Leery. "My office, all of you."

"Uh-oh," Leery whispered. "Mommy's mad."

Dru rolled her eyes and brushed by him. Angie followed her with a wry twist to her lips, leaving Puriel and Leery standing alone.

"For what it's worth," said Puriel. "Chief Smith's got more than one loose screw."

"You don't say?" Leery lips twitched.

"Yes. He thinks supernaturals are a disease...a cancer."

"I think I've seen this movie," Leery said and lost his fight with a grin. He patted Puriel on the shoulder and led him into Van Helsing's office.

Epatha sat flickering in her chair, though the frequency of the flicker had decreased. She stared down at the top of her desk.

"Lieutenant," said Puriel. "If I might begin by offering my apologies about—"

"No, listen. Chief Magnussen is behind us. You all did the right thing. Smith is angry because he feels like you encroached on his turf. He likes orderly little operations where everything goes as planned." She shrugged.

"That's why he was promoted out of the way." She turned her gaze on Leery. "Antagonizing him, though, is stupid. What we—"

"Hey, I just call 'em like I see 'em, Lieu. You know that."

"—need to do is hash this mess out"—she nodded to show she'd heard Leery—"and come up with a plan to get out in front of it. You see, Oriscoe? Mommy's not really mad." She quirked a grin at him as his cheeks colored, and as she did so, her flickering finally stopped. "So, what the hell is going on?"

Puriel cleared his throat.

"Sorry," muttered Van Helsing.

"It's nothing," said the angel with an expression that said otherwise.

"Let's lay it out," said Ice. "It starts with Raguel in an alley."

"Right. And you suggested the Gardeners as a possible avenue for following the snacks," said Dru.

Ice nodded. "Yeah, while we were waiting on the ME's analysis."

"And where is she on that score?" asked Van Helsing.

"She found a dairy-based substance but has had trouble narrowing it down," said Dru. "We met with Dawn"—she nodded at the woman—"and she suggested we talk to the Little Gray Men because of the recent fracas with the Gardeners."

Dawn nodded. "They had a turf dispute."

Leery grinned. "We know a little about those."

"The Big Gray Man told us about the secret ingredients of several other curdle crews in the City. Based on Liz's report—about the dairy component—we ruled out who we could, then we went to see the Gardeners, and after a little fracas of our own, we brought some of them in." Dru cocked her head to the side. "They gave us the names of a quartet of Leprechauns, but before we could do more than take a sip of coffee, angelfire flashed in Tompkins Square."

Puriel cleared his throat. "It was not numinous fire."

"Right, but we didn't know that then," said Leery. "Dawn suggested we visit with Puriel about that, to see who might be running around spreading the Wrath of God."

Puriel grimaced and shook his head.

"But instead, we find Mack—one of the four names we got from the Gardeners—pretending to be righteous. And *he* gives us the Svartalfar thread to follow."

"How much do you want to bet some crisis is about to pop off and it turns out there's a Svartalfr behind it all?" asked Ice.

"Sucker's bet," murmured Leery. "So, we're left with either the Gardeners or the Leprechauns pulling the strings."

"Or someone else. Who gains from all this? And who is being hurt?"

"The Little Gray Men took it on the chin."

"Yes," said Ice. "And the Leprechauns will end up without Mack, one way or another, so theoretically, they'll be weakened by this."

"The Gardeners gave up a few of their own," said Dawn.

"Did they?" asked Van Helsing.

The detective shrugged. "Sure. They lose Jenkor the Rake and Reknad the Machete."

"Right. Those two who supposedly screwed up so much that Arvidar would just turn them over to us." Leery shook his head.

Dawn frowned. "Yeah, that doesn't fit."

"And they were told to *cooperate*, to feed us the Leprechaun names."

"By Arvidar," added Epatha.

"Both gangs lose some high-ranking players. Both gangs come out looking like they snitched." Ice shook his head.

"That doesn't fit, either," said Dawn.

"Follow the sins," murmured Puriel.

"The sins? Really?" asked Leery.

"Why Raguel?" the angel asked. "Why now?"

Leery shrugged. "Why not now? What makes Raguel special?"

"Besides being an angel, you mean?" asked Puriel. "Think about it. An *angel* is the first case in the war on snacks? An *angel* leads you to gnomes who point you at the leprechauns—and they pretend to be angels when killing a whole whack of gnomes—who point you at the Svartalfar?"

"It does kind of seem like a progression."

"Sure, it does," said Puriel. "And why start with an angel as the victim?"

"Look at the evil snack slinger," said Ice. "Corrupting even the angels."

"Right! And who's to blame?"

"Those dirty dark-siders," said Dawn with a grimace.

"Yeah, okay," said Leery. "But dark-siders seem to be cooperating with the scheme."

"And why would they?" asked Puriel. "What currency could buy such self-betrayals?"

"I'm not sure I like the phrase 'dark-siders,'" said Dru. "And any answer we come up with is pure speculation."

"Then let's ask people who wouldn't be speculating," said Puriel. "If you can spare the time, I know a Svartalfr who will speak plainly—the owner of the Nidavellir bar in Hel's Kitchen. Dawn and I can…gaze upon other vistas." He quirked a grin at the Nagual and held out his hand. Smiling, Dawn took it, then Puriel snapped them away.

13

Leery backed the car out into traffic, ignoring the shriek of tires and cacophony of car horns, spun the wheel with one hand, slurping station-house coffee from the mug Puriel had given him and grimacing at the taste. "There's something to that holy water thing, Dru. I'm telling you."

"Tap water, Leery. Then someone prays over it."

"Maybe it's filtered?"

"Naw, man," said Ice. "You should listen to your partner."

"Spring water, then. From a well under Puriel's house."

"New York tap water," said Dru. "From the treatment plant on the Hudson. You know, where we found those bodies a month or so ago."

"Hmm. Well, something is sure better."

"Better than that battery acid from the house? Yeah, *anything* is better than that."

"You've got a point."

"You know how to get to the Nidavellir?" asked Ice from the back seat. "I'm afraid to look."

"Hey, it's in Hel's Kitchen, and before you ask, yes, I know it well. I *grew up* here, Ice."

"Nidavellir, man. 9th and 54th."

"Yeah, I got it, I got it." Leery twitched the car through slower moving traffic, and Ice groaned from the back. "Though it's a little early in the day for a nightclub. Are they even open this time of the afternoon? And more importantly, do they have good coffee?"

"I'm sure we can feed your demon after we talk to Puriel's friend."

Leery grunted and concentrated on shifting the Crown Vic around like a Formula One driver for a few minutes. He pulled the car up onto the curb at the corner with a grunt, pointing down the hood of the car at the four-story building in front of them. Neon beer signs festooned the transoms above the wood-framed glass doors that wrapped the first floor. The word 'Nidavellir' was etched into the transom glass above the closest door, and two small black signs repeated the name facing both 9th Street and 54th. A rusty steel beam served as a lintel above the wall of glass. "Look, I found it without anyone holding my hand or nothing."

"Will wonders never cease," said Ice, getting out. "And we made it alive."

"I keep telling you, Ice. There's no replacement for experience when it comes to driving in Manhattan."

"Sanity would be a good start."

Leery turned away without a reply and scanned the nearby businesses. "No Starbucks in sight," he grunted. "And they say there's one on every corner."

Ice stepped around him and peered at the door. "It says here they have forty-eight beers on tap."

"Yeah, sure. *Beer.* I bet it doesn't say one word about coffee…"

A tall, slender man stepped up inside the door. His dusky gray skin seemed almost blue, standing, as he was, in the shadowy interior. His hair was blue-black and hung to his shoulders. His ears swooped gracefully back and ended in points that looked sharp enough to cut paper. He grimaced at them and pointed to the sign next to the door handle.

"Uh-oh," said Leery. "Someone's grumpy."

"It says they don't open until three," said Ice.

"That's okay, I brought my skeleton key." Leery slid his badge out of his pocket and slapped it on the glass, then tilted his head a little and smiled at the Svartalfr. "Open up in the name of the law!" he called with a wink.

The dark elf scowled at him, then extended his hand, turned the lock with glacial slowness, and cracked the door an inch. "What?" he snapped in clipped tones.

"And a good afternoon to you, as well," said Leery. "We need to talk to you. Got the coffee on yet?"

The Svartalfr's eyes narrowed to the barest of slits, but not before Leery noticed they were all black—sclera, irises, pupils alike. "What do you want? Where's your warrant?"

"We need to talk, uh…" Leery looked at Dru. "Nidi Glumrsen?"

"Nithi Gloomersen," the Svartalfr corrected. "That's not a D, it's an Eth, and that's an acute over the U. You could at least *try* to pronounce it correctly."

"Okay, Correctly. Listen, I'm Leery Oriscoe, this is my partner, Dru Nogan, and this guy here goes by the slightly blasphemous moniker of Ice Cofy. Don't worry, though, his last name is spelled differently from the drink, so it makes it okay."

Nithi turned a flat-eyed expression on Ice, then turned toward Dru and froze. After a moment of staring, he nodded. "Cousin," he said.

"Hello," said Dru.

"Oh, you two know each other?" asked Leery with a confused smile.

"No, dolt," murmured Nithi. "But we are cousins, nonetheless." He turned his haughty stare on Leery once more. "I am one of Hel's Chosen. She is merely of another branch of the family."

Leery turned his gaze on Dru and arched an eyebrow.

"Metaphorically speaking," she said.

"Uh, sure," said Leery. "Anyway, Correctly…about that coffee?"

"I have no coffee for you!" snapped the black elf, starting to push the door closed.

Dru slipped in front of Leery. "We are here on official business, Mr. Gloomerson. Puriel sent us."

He glared over her for a moment, his hostile gaze burning. "Call me Nithi," he said after a few moments and stepped back. "Come in."

The interior of the bar, though swathed in shadows, conveyed a sense of warmth and welcome. The plaster walls were dressed up with mellow wood panels and Viking-themed decorations, along with the standard "neighborhood bar" motifs—beer signs, license plates, pennants, chalkboard menus, strings of Christmas tree lights, and brass—lots of brass.

"Nice place," said Leery. "Love what you've done with it."

"I suppose a Svartalfar bar should be dark and smoky? Done in black and gray?" sneered Nithi.

"Hey, no offense, chum. I meant what I said."

Nithi turned to Dru without another word. "Why did Puriel refer you to me, cousin?"

"We're on a case. A case that doesn't make sense."

"And?" said the dark elf, arching one eyebrow.

"Those axes real, man?" asked Ice, gazing at the arms and armor decorating the barback.

"Antiques," grunted Nithi with a dismissive glance.

"*And*," said Dru, "the case seems to be painting a grim picture of those of us from the 'wrong side of the tracks.'"

Nithi frowned.

"It gets worse," said Leery and outlined the case. "The latest brush strokes are aimed at your people specifically."

"Who accuses us?"

"A leprechaun."

Nithi pulled his chin back, confusion chiseled into his features. "A leprechaun?"

"And a Leprechaun. One of the leaders of the gang. Says they helped you out in a turf dispute, and that your people returned the favor by letting him know the Little Gray Men snitched the Leprechauns out."

Nithi's lip curled. "I don't traffic with the gangs. Not any longer."

"No, of course not," said Dru. "What we are confused about is this: if all this is a setup, then why would the Gardeners and the Leprechauns go along with casting the blame on themselves?"

"Not to mention acting like snitches."

Nithi swung up a section of the bar and walked behind it, frowning. He pulled a pot of coffee from under the bar and set up four mugs, then filled them with sable velvet. "I have nothing to ruin this with," he said.

Dru sighed and reached for a cup.

"Don't mind her," said Leery. "She takes it with a pound-and-a-half of sugar." He shuddered. "I drink it like the universe intended it to be drank."

Nithi sneered at him but nodded. "As to your case, gnomes..."

"Yeah, I know," said Leery. "More mischievous than 'dark,' right?"

Nithi nodded. "We certainly wouldn't consider them cousins."

"And leprechauns?" asked Cofy, sipping his coffee.

Nithi rocked his hand from side to side. "Questionable. Most fit the mischief-maker role better than, say a malevolent one, though others lend a darker cast to their exploits."

"So, your people wouldn't consider them almost-cousins?" asked Leery after a sip of coffee. "Hey! This is really good! Even better than Puriel's."

"No," said Nithi. "We view both races as something akin to poseurs. Yes, they run in packs"—he grimaced and tipped his head toward Leery—"your pardon. They run in gangs of miscreants, selling their snacks, fighting over meaningless street corners, but their exploits rarely lead to more than a few bruises, a few bumps on the head."

"Which races do you consider truly dark?" asked Ice.

"Races? Come now, Detective. Surely, we are beyond gross generalizations? Detective Nogan's people come from one of the so-called 'dark realms,' yet here she is, acting on the side of law and order. I'm nothing more than an innkeeper, a seller of beer. Detective Leery's Pack would have been considered evil not so many decades past, yet here he is as well."

"I see your point. We're all just people."

"Correct."

"Then what organizations would you consider truly dark?"

"From my realm? *Hel's Englar* of the Svartalfar, of course. The Duhkkalfar crew called the *Oolfur*. The *Plowir Medn* from the Myrkalfar. Then there's the—"

"Uh..." said Leery, scribbling in his pad. "Can you give me a second to..."

"Hel's Angels from the black elves, the Wolves from the dark elves, the Blue Men from the murky elves," said Nithi with a grimace. "Easier?"

Leery shrugged. "Much. I wasn't aware there were so many different kinds of non-glowy elves."

Nithi rolled his eyes. "Then there's the Zombie mafia, of course. The Dead Set. The Unseelie Court has numerous groups. There may be a kobold gang or two. And the goblins and hobgoblins, of course. The mutens, the shadowen. mwellrets..." Nithi shrugged. "I'm no expert in other races. However, of my people, I can't see them trafficking with the gnomes or the leprechauns. No, my people would snuff them out if they grew noisome."

"Our witness claimed the Svartalfar owed a debt of honor to the Leprechauns. We assumed there was a specific gang involved," said Dru.

Nithi frowned and his eyes blazed. "If so, it would be those animals in the *Utanathkomanti*—the Outsiders. They reject Svartalfar culture and mores, embracing anarchy chaos."

"These *Utanath*... These Outsiders," said Leery. "How can we find them?"

Nithi cocked his head to the side and gave Leery a narrow-eyed, assessing look. "That wouldn't be wise."

"Hey, pal, not much I do in this job could be considered wise."

Nithi shrugged. "Let me rephrase, then. That would be spectacularly *un*wise." He glanced at Dru. "It would be far better to speak with one of the *Hel's Englar*. Perhaps they will intervene in your stead." He tossed his blue-black hair. "But on second thought, even that is a waste of time. The *Utanathkomanti* don't even want contact with their own kind, let alone other races. They worship *Owraythu*—a dark old goddess whose very name means pure 'chaos.' Her twin brother is *Mirkur*, 'darkness' and he's the deity of both darkness and anarchy." He shook his head. "No, on reflection, it is impossible, what this witness claims."

Leery treated him to a single nod. "Okay, but if it's not your people…"

Nithi's brow furrowed, and he crossed one arm over his chest, resting his other elbow in the cup of his palm, his other hand stroking his chin. "There is *something*…a vague tickle…" He grimaced. "A portion of a conversation I must have overheard here at the bar. Something about a group of...what were they? Orcs?" He shook his head, dropping his arms to his sides and plucking at his cotton shirt tails. "No, that's not it," he muttered. "Shanka?" He shook his head and squinted down at the bar. "No, but *like* the Shanka...a created race..." He jerked his chin up and snapped his fingers. "Yes! Redcaps!"

"Goblins," said Dru in a breathy voice. She turned a wide-eyed stare on Leery. "Like the GC..."

"Oh, shit..." he murmured. "How sure are you about this?"

"Very, now that I've recalled the conversation. My memory is very robust once I find the thread." Nithi slapped his palm on the bar. "Yes. Two muten and a hobgoblin were arguing about a gang of Redcaps who seemed to be encroaching on their protection racket in Brooklyn."

"Their names?" asked Leery, his pen poised over his notebook.

Nithi shook his head. "No, I don't know that. This is a bar, after all. No names are required."

"How about the name of the Redcap gang?" asked Ice.

"That's the thing that made me remember," said Nithi. "The hob kept calling them the

Black Elves. The muten called them the *Owthechktur*. It means 'the unknown,' but I wondered at the time why a group of goblins would adopt the 'Black Elves' as even a nickname for their gang."

Leery glanced at Dru, then wrote down the information. He polished off his mug of coffee and grinned, though it lacked its normal good cheer. "Thanks for the information, Mr. Gloomersen. *And* the good coffee. I'll be back for more of the latter, and you can count on that."

Nithi flicked his head to the side. "We're open from three in the afternoon to four in the morning, seven days a week."

"And," said Leery fishing out his card. "If you ever find yourself in a jam…" He flipped the card over and wrote his cell number on the back. "Give this number a call. We owe you one."

Nithi flicked his head again, but he took the card. He followed them to the door, closing the door behind them and turning the lock with a snap.

Leery slid into the driver's seat but then sat there, staring at nothing, one foot still on the baking concrete. Ice climbed in on the passenger side, grumbling something about people who welch on bets, and Dru crabbed into the center of the backseat and leaned forward to hunch between them.

"Penny," she said, looking at Leery.

"How long until we're supposed to meet Puriel and Dawn?" Leery murmured.

"About an hour and a half," said Ice. "You got somewhere to be?"

"Yeah," he said. "1PP. Let's go talk to Evie."

"Evie?"

"Yvonne Evans," said Dru. "Leery's old partner. She works OC."

"Ah. Good idea," said Ice.

"I'll call her," said Dru. "You head to downtown."

14

Evie beat them to the Starbucks, but this time she hadn't bothered to hide the tray of coffee. She grinned at Leery and slid two *trenta* cups toward him. "Seven sugars," she said sweetly.

"You'd better hope not," said Leery with a grin.

"Aw, come on, McGruff," she said with a twinkle in her eye. "Expand your horizons."

"McGruff?" asked Ice.

"It's a long story," said Leery.

Evie chuckled. "Not really. Leery's a wolf, right? Well, he has this nemesis-relationship with one of our CSI techs—a fine demon named Jenn DuBrava Hinton. He started teasing her about the size of her feet, and, well, she started calling him by the names of famous dogs. It kind of caught on with certain people, and bingo—"

"Cute," said Leery.

"—everyone at 1PP was doing it."

"Her feet really *are* huge. The size of school busses. And, to be honest, she said something like 'School bus, my foot!' and I said, 'They're not *that* big.'"

"Yeah, I bet," said Ice. "You got a thing for name-calling, eh?"

Leery hit him with his best "who me?" look.

"And it wasn't so much that conversation that spurred her on," said Evie. "It was the pictures of school buses you put up all over the place. And the school bus birthday card."

"Don't forget the cake with tanks on it."

"Right. That, too." Evie grinned. "Anyway, you earned it, Laika."

"Sure, sure," said Leery before burying his nose in one of the *trentas* and taking a big whiff. He took a sip and smiled. "I knew you wouldn't ruin good coffee."

Evie winked at him.

"So..." said Dru. "Ever hear of a gang of Redcaps called either the Black Elves or the *Owthechktur*? Or maybe the Unknown?"

Evie grimaced—glancing first at Ice, then at Dru, and finally, Leery—then nodded sourly. "Why?"

"We're on the Raguel case."

"And the Unknown are involved?"

"Maybe." Leery shrugged. "Probably."

Evie wrinkled her brow. "That's not good."

"No?" asked Dru. "Why?"

Evie turned her head a bit, as though she were checking to see if anyone were close. "They're strong, organized, and *growing*—either by absorbing smaller gangs or crushing them under heel. They're like Teflon, too. When there is enough evidence to arrest anyone linked to them, the suspect somehow avoids prosecution. Usually, there's another crime that casts a reasonable doubt elsewhere."

Leery grunted. "Angelfire."

"What?" Evie's brow crinkled even more.

"Later. Go on," said Dru.

"There's chatter… Some say they're protected."

"By who?" asked Ice.

Evie shrugged. "There's no evidence that there *is* any protection, let alone pointing in any particular direction. It's more like an indication of frustration that no one can make a case that sticks."

"Maybe…" murmured Leery, his gaze resting on a point above their heads.

"Maybe what?"

He dropped his gaze to Evie's. "You still tight with the Ceebie OC goons? The wonks that do math and stuff with springsheets?"

"Spreadsheets. Sure."

"Reach out to them and see what they know about these Redcaps?" For once, there was no hint of a smile, sarcastic or otherwise, on Leery's face. "Where do they get their money, for instance?"

"I can do that," said Evie. "Though…"

"I know it's a sticky topic to ask about right now."

"Right. In the meantime, let me give you a trail to start down. The Unknown aren't really a gang—at least not in the context of a street gang. They're more of an organization, an alliance."

"An alliance of what?" asked Ice.

"Street gangs, petty criminals, snack dealers. They're tiny compared to the Zombie mafia, but they're growing, like I said. They're ruthless and ultra-violent when pushed. Where the gnomes might have a few fights, the Unknown will murder entire families, burn down apartment buildings."

Leery looked at Dru. "Drop angelfire on a gnome gang in the middle of a park?"

"Well, it wouldn't be numinous fire, but yeah, something like that."

"And this misdirection thing they do...would hiring a leprechaun to attack said gang of gnomes in broad daylight while using a reality warp to make it look like angelfire fit the bill?"

"I can't think of a scheme that better exemplifies their mindset."

"Ah. And you have a string for us to pull on?"

Evie grinned. "Sure do. One of my CIs received an invitation to join the Unknown. And by invitation, I mean her brothers are in the hospital after falling down a flight of stairs, getting up, dusting themselves off, climbing back up and falling down again, then repeating the process a few more times."

"Do you have a name for us, or are we going to have to haul you around with us?"

"No time for that," said Evie. "I'm in court this afternoon. My CI's Alentina Washburn. I'll text you her details. She works for the Locus Cynosure's office."

"Better text her," said Leery, hooking his thumb toward Dru. "I'm no good with these things."

"Riiight," said Evie with a slow smile. "Is he *still* trying to pull that?"

"Every minute of every day," said Dru.

"Speaking of minutes," he said. "We've got to meet Puriel in a few of them."

15

Leery bumped the front tires of the Crown Vic up on the curb, narrowly missing a fire hydrant, then goosed the accelerator. The dark blue car jumped onto the sidewalk in front of a cream-colored building with a brown sign reading "Brooklyn Emerald" above the door and a stack of paper coffee cups in the window. "We've got a few minutes until we meet Puriel and Dawn, right?"

Ice leaned over the seat and looked at Dru. "Does he seriously spend his day going from coffee shop to coffee shop?"

"Hey, sometimes I get coffee from the precinct, too."

Ice shook his head. "Knock yourself out, man. But I got to say that you might need help."

"Nah. Coffee's light. I can carry three or four cups all by myself." Leery flashed his patented I'm-so-cute grin. "You two want anything?"

"Naw, man, I'm good," said Ice, while Dru only grinned and rolled her eyes. "Listen, Oriscoe, Puriel's building is right next door. The one with the gray on the ground floor. We're meeting him up in the penthouse."

"Right, but I'll only be a minute. In fact..." He peered into the coffee shop, then grinned. "Here comes my order now."

"What, do they have an app, too?" asked Dru.

"Yeah, sort of." Leery hopped out and opened the door for the pretty woman balancing four cups of coffee. He slipped her a twenty, then beckoned Dru and Ice with his shoulder, holding the four cups squished together between his palms and taking an unsteady sip from the first cup. "Come on, slowpokes. We might as well head up."

By the time the elevator disgorged them in the marble lobby of the penthouse suite, Leery had crumpled two of the cups of coffee and dropped them into the waste receptacle in the corner. He drank from the third cup, smiling from ear to ear. "Just as good as Starbucks, so about half as good as Puriel's, but it's got its own flair."

"You're gonna hurt yourself, drinking like that."

"Nah. Big bladder," said Leery, taking another gulp.

Shaking his head, Ice walked across to the oak double doors and rapped his fingers on the right one.

"Come on in!" shouted Puriel through the door. "It's unlocked!"

The foyer was paneled in a rich oak that matched the doors, the floor's black granite tiles the size of a car door. It opened on a grand living room space replete with a grand piano, a harpsichord, and a pipe organ, of all things. The furnishings practically bled opulence—leather-swathed Baroque chairs and sofas, oversized hand-carved moldings, twisted columns, cassini, and elaborate candelabra on wide wooden side tables. The far wall was done entirely of glass, without any visible framing, and two sections of that stood open, leading to the largest roof-top garden Leery had ever seen.

Large trees grew as if it were perfectly natural for them to grow from a roof in the middle of the concrete jungle that was New York City. Grass carpeted the entire roof, with shrubbery arranged to create outdoor rooms of sorts. An outdoor kitchen stabbed into the garden like a sword-thrust from the glass-wall of the interior kitchen. The centerpiece, however, was a beautiful sculpted pool and the golden fish swimming within it.

"Nice place," said Leery. "If you go in for this kind of thing. Personally, I go for—"

"Cramped cracker box style apartments on the Upper West Side," said Dru, hiding a grin.

"Oh, you've heard this one already?" asked Leery, smiling with one side of his mouth.

"Not unless you count every day for eternity."

"Well... I guess I need some new material."

"That ain't all you need," grumbled Ice. "A wardrobe consultant would help."

Leery glanced down at his brown suit coat, his lime green tie, his pale blue shirt, and gray pants. "What's wrong with this?"

"Incredible," murmured Ice as he turned away and strode toward the outdoor couch and chairs grouping where Dawn and Puriel sat. The black-haired man sitting opposite them turned his head as Cofy approached.

His skin was deeply golden in the manner of the Mexica. He had a black painted band that stretched from his brows to the tops of his high cheekbones. Yellow bands of paint, about half the thickness of the black band, bordered the black on either side. He nodded, and Ice nodded back as they came around the couch.

"Detectives, meet Tezcatlipoca, the Smoking Mirror," said Puriel. "Tezy, meet detectives Leery Oriscoe, Ice Cofy, and the belle of the ball, Dru Nogan."

Tezy's gaze flicked to them each in turn, but when it came to rest on Dru's face, he smiled. "Come now, Puriel. You know who she is." He stood and bowed to Dru. "Your Grace."

She smiled and dipped a curtsy back. "Your Excellence."

"Come. You must sit next to me," said Tezy, moving down the couch. "Tell me of things in Gehenna."

"Perhaps another time, Your Majesty."

He waved the title away. "Call me Tezy. So few observe the old forms."

"Very true," she said. "And I'll call you Tezy if you call me Dru."

He grinned and sank to the cushions. "Done." He patted the couch next to him.

Dru sat down, with a quick glance at Dawn, while Leery and Ice found chairs and brought them over. After everything was settled, Puriel leaned forward and smiled. "Tezy has a theory." He nodded at the Aztec.

"I believe your case centers on something bigger than gangs of ruffians pointing fingers at one another," said Tezy. "These incidents...these *confessions*...have the feel of a sacrifice."

"And if anyone would know..." said Leery with a grin.

Tezy grinned back. "There may be something to what you say."

"We found out something ourselves," said Dru. "From Nithi Gloomersen."

Puriel nodded.

"There is a band of Redcaps moving into the City from Brooklyn," said Leery. "They go by some unpronounceable Norse word that means the Unknown."

"Goblins," said Puriel with a sigh.

"And others, but the main push seems to be coming from the Redcaps."

"Ah," said Tezy. "Then it makes more sense."

"How so?" asked Ice.

"They require a sacrifice"—he shrugged—"though not necessarily blood sacrifice, in order to join them. It could be money, or power, or anything important to the prospective new member."

"Then these confessions, these misdirections, are the price of admission," said Puriel.

"I'd bet my mirror on it," said Tezy, tapping the polished onyx on his chest.

"One of my old partners is going to text us the name of a CI who has been invited to join the Unknown by way of putting her family in the hospital. She may have more information for us."

"Redcaps," murmured Puriel tugging his lip. "Returning to our previous discussion then, immediately following the GC's speech calling for a war on snacks, the Redcaps overdose an angel to point the finger at the various snack dealers—"

"Who happen to have territory across the river from Brooklyn."

"Just so," said Puriel with a nod. "Which will create a vacuum of supply when the inevitable crackdown comes."

"There'll be a power vacuum, too," said Ice. "That seems convenient."

"Doesn't it, though," said Tezy.

"All of this so the Unknown can move into Manhattan and sell curdles?" asked Dawn with a dubious expression on her face.

"Seems like a touch of overkill," said Leery.

"And what does the GC get out of it?"

Leery pumped his shoulders. "Money for his reelection campaign? Looking good to the citizenry? More power in certain circles?"

"Soundbites that get his name in the news," said Ice. "He gets to look like he's taking a tough stance against crime and addiction, but he's not really doing anything."

"And, perhaps," said Tezy with a slow grin, "his reform isn't as complete as he'd have us believe. Maybe his old loyalties are still strong, just buried from the public eye."

"Hey, he *is* a politician, after all," said Leery with a grimace. "There are probably quite a few hidden things about him."

Wearing a subtle smile, Tezy inclined his head and winked at Leery. "Of that, there is no doubt."

Leery's phone buzzed and he tossed it to Dru. "It's going to explode, I think."

She rolled her eyes and swept away the lock screen. "Ah. Evie's CI can see us if we head on over."

16

Leery pulled into an empty parking space beneath an elm tree growing from the sidewalk on Pierrepont Street in Brooklyn. Dru arched an eyebrow at him. "Hey, a guy doesn't want to be *too* predictable, right?"

"Come on," said Ice, sliding out the back door.

"Eager, isn't he?"

"Yeah," said Dru. "He gets car sick."

Leery nodded out the front windshield. "Kind of a nice neighborhood for a CI."

"Yeah," said Dru. "But it takes all kinds, and this CI works for the Locus Cynosure, remember. Evie *is* in OC."

They got out and crossed the road to a corner building painted red and brown and rode the creaking elevator to the third floor. When they stepped out, Ice twitched his chin toward 3C.

"What's her name again?" he asked.

"Alentina Washburn," said Leery. "And remember, she's Evie's CI, so go easy."

"I'm always easy, player. Unless they want it some other way." Ice lifted his hand and knocked on the door, then crossed his hands in front of him and leaned in to peer through the peephole. "Someone's moving around at least."

The door opened to reveal a short-haired woman. "Yes?" she asked in a voice that held a soft Texas twang.

"Alentina Washburn?" asked Ice.

"Yes. Who are you?"

"Cops," said Leery.

"Let us in, Alentina," said Ice.

She stepped back, her face carefully blank. "You're cops?"

"Detectives," said Dru. "Supernatural Inquisitors Squad. We're the ones Yvonne Evans texted you about."

"And I'm with Spectral Victims, but we're here about your invitation."

"My invitation." She stepped back again, and three detectives crowded into her foyer.

"Sure," said Leery. "From the ugly guys with red caps?"

"Yes," she said in a breathy exhalation. "I don't think of it as an invitation." Alentina turned and walked into the small living room. "Come in," she muttered. "Have a seat." She drifted to a well-loved easy chair and sat on its edge. "I've told Detective Evans everything I could think of."

Leery crossed the room and peered into a glass case containing a series of antique mortar and pestles, beakers, vials, and obscure scientific-looking gizmos. He raised an eyebrow at the display, then glanced at Alentina. "What is it you do?"

"I...work for His Excellency, the Locus Cynosure."

"That's what Evie said. In what capacity?" asked Leery.

"I'm a...special assistant."

"Ah," Oriscoe said. "And what does that mean?"

Alentina shrugged. "I'm a disciple of Hermes Trismegistus in the Great Tradition."

"Uh...sure," said Leery.

"She means she's an alchemist," said Ice with a sly grin. "Special assistant, huh?

What's His Excellency need with an alchemist?"

Alentina looked at her hands, which were strangling one another in her lap. "I... I can't say. My oath..."

"Ever have any dealings with the GC?" asked Leery. "You or His Excellency?"

Alentina shook her head. "Look, when the Unknown started sniffing around, I did my duty. I called the cops, and I'm cooperating with Detective Evans"—she raised her gaze and stared at Ice—"*about the Unknown*. What they've done to my family. I'm not going to talk to you about the LC. His Excellency has broken no laws. Not even close."

"If it's innocent, why is it secret?" asked Leery.

"It..." Alentina shook her head. "It's personal, and that's all I'm going to say about it."

Leery turned to Dru. "Do you think it's illegal to finance a campaign on transmuted lead?"

Alentina chuckled. "That's ludicrous."

"If this were fiction, that's what all this would be about. You'd have discovered the formula for changing lead to gold, and the Redcaps would've found you out. They'd be—"

"What a soap opera," said Alentina with a chuckle. "You've got quite an imagination."

"I get that a lot," said Leery.

"Why are they interested in you?" asked Dru in a quiet voice "The Redcaps, I mean. What makes you so special to them? They've put in quite an effort to snare you, no?"

Alentina's chuckle died. "Well, it's not transmutation." She looked down at her lap again. "Cynosure Endy has...special needs."

"Uh-huh," said Leery. "I'll bet he does."

"Not like that!" snapped Washburn. "*Medicinal* needs. Alchemical needs."

Leery looked to Dru and lifted his shoulders.

"Let's leave that for now," said Dru. "And as long as it isn't germane to our case, we can leave it forever."

"What is your case?"

"Raguel," said Ice. "And why the snack slingers across the river are acting so damn weird."

"We figure it has something to do with the Unknown, and since they seem so interested in you..."

"Yes, well, I wish they weren't!"

"I'm sure," said Dru. "Why do you think they are?"

"It's obvious, isn't it? I'm a high-order alchemist. They must want me to cook up some new snack recipes for them." She glanced at Leery. "Or maybe they believe in transmutation, too."

Leery glanced at the cabinet full of antiques. "So far, there's no evidence they care about slinging snacks. In fact, they seem perfectly willing to scuttle the whole industry to serve their needs."

Alentina lifted her chin. "Maybe they want to clear the boards, to get rid of all the competition."

"Maybe," said Ice with a shrug. "Tell us what you know about them."

"*Nothing*," moaned Alentina. "I was approached by a goblin in the park. He said he had a proposition for me, and I told him to get lost. I thought... Well, it doesn't matter what I thought. He just grinned at me and walked away. Later that evening, I learned my brother was in the hospital. On the way there, another goblin slid into my cab at a light—the cabbie *let* him in—and said he had a proposition for me, and that this time, I probably wanted to hear him out."

"And? Did you listen to him?"

"Of course! He said he represented the Unknown and that they needed a woman with my skills. I asked him what skills they needed and what they wanted me to do, but he wouldn't tell me that. He gave the cabbie a new destination, and I waited until the light changed, then I jumped out and ran."

"And another brother fell down some stairs?"

She nodded. "At the hospital this time. He'd been visiting my other brother."

"Then what?" asked Ice.

"I called Endy, and he connected me with Detective Evans via the commissioner."

"Have you seen any other goblins since then?"

Alentina shook her head. "But I've been getting messages." She got up and crossed to her rolltop desk, shuffled some papers out of the way, and came back with a card on vellum stock. The message written on the card flowed in a calligraphic script that seemed at the same time hideous and beautiful. "It's a secret recipe from my order. The *alkahest*—the universal solvent."

Leery shrugged.

"A powerful chemical able to dissolve just about anything. Skin, for instance."

"They want you to make this solvent for them?"

"No, if they have this, they have a Hermetic alchemist of sufficient skill to make it, as well."

"Then why—"

"It's a threat," said Ice in a grim tone. "Join us, or we'll use this instead of stairs next time."

Alentina nodded, then burst into tears.

"What are you supposed to do to contact them?" asked Dru. "Do you have a name? A phone number?"

Washburn swiped at her tears with the back of her hand. "There's a bar in Greenpoint called the Saint Julian Bar and Grill. They play that heavy metal music all the time there. I'm supposed to ask for Kleshas Findfault."

"Saint Julian's, huh?" mused Ice.

Alentina nodded and sniffed.

"Why? What's so special about Saint Julian?" asked Dru.

"He's the patron saint of murderers, among other things," said Leery.

"Yeah, but he repented," said Ice. "Somehow, I think these Redcaps missed that part of the story." He glanced at Alentina. "Sit tight, Ms. Washburn, and try not to worry.

We'll go visit these dumbos and see if we can't set things right."

17

Saint Julian's Bar and Grill had no sign, and the nondescript building had only a flat black door set in the middle of a flat black wall facing Manhattan Avenue. A big iron padlock secured the door. Leery rattled the black door to Saint Julian's and grimaced at the building next door—the Rio de Janeiro Restaurant and Deli, its brazen carnival paint scheme making the bar seem even more obscure.

"Closed?" asked Ice.

"Yeah. Not very hospitable—they don't even have a sign showing when they *will* open."

"Hmph," grunted an old woman coming out of the Rio de Janeiro. "Those little bastards are always there. Living there, probably."

"Oh?"

The old woman turned her bright-eyed stare on Leery. "Yeah. They're some kind of *quadrilha*, too. *Criadores de problemas!*

Always flashing their red hats at a woman minding her own business. *Bandidos,* I tell you."

"I take it you live nearby?"

The woman hawked and spat, then pointed across the street with a gnarled hand. "Third floor. Everyone's scared of them. Scared they'll get murdered or worse."

"But not you?" Leery asked with a smile.

"No, not me," said the woman. "I'm the last of my family, and all I've got to look forward to is years of pain." She put her hand on her hip. "Rheumatoid Arthritis, the doctors call it. I call it a *bastardo de rato. Coisa do caralho*!" She hawked and spat again. "If not for Maria and Joao, I'd starve to death in the bad times."

"Maria and Joao?" asked Ice.

"The Antunes. They own it," she said, hooking her thumb at the restaurant. "When I'm *lutando contra o monstro ruim,* sweet Maria brings me food. When I'm good enough, I *atravessar a rua* to save her *o problema.*"

"And these 'troublemakers' who run the bar?" asked Ice. "You ever see them in the Rio?"

"*Não.* They play their *barulho* until *a hora do diabo,* and by that time, they're all *bêbado e chapado.* They never eat, them. Drink, *sim, como os peixes.* Sleep all day, *fazer barulho* all night."

Ice lifted his chin. "Know how we can get in there? We tried the door."

"*Sim, volta.* Ring the bell back there."

"*Obrigado,*" said Ice. The old woman nodded and made her way to the crosswalk. "She says go around back and ring the bell."

"You speak Portuguese, Ice?"

"Carnival is a bag of fun, wolfman. I get down there every year. You should try it."

"Maybe I will," said Leery with a glance at Dru. "Maybe I'll go for Christmas."

"I'm telling you, man…go for Carnival. You're missing out, otherwise. It's five days in February, too. Exchange the cold snow for warm fun."

Leery shrugged. "I'll check it out. But come on, let's go around back like the old lady said. See if we can rouse one of those troublemakers."

They turned the corner onto Clay Street and then ducked into the alley behind the Rio De Janeiro. A black-painted back door stood at the end of the alley, and an intercom box with a buzzer hung on the wall next to it just as the old woman had said. A sign hung from the door, announcing in bright red letters that all deliveries had to wait until after six pm. Leery grinned and jabbed the button with his thumb and leaned on it. Upstairs, a ringing akin to a fire alarm started.

After a few moments, heavy footfalls thudded down a set of steps, and the heavy deadbolts securing the door snapped back. "The sign says no deliveries before six!" The door jerked open and a short figure bustled out. He looked like an old man—long stringy gray hair cascading down from beneath a blood-red cap, a hatchet of a nose set between beady all-black eyes. He had pointed ears that swept back from his cheeks, their pointed tips tucked under the headband of his red cap. His arms seemed too long for his torso, as did his knobby-kneed legs. He wore metal-wrapped boots, black leather trousers, and not a thing else. "What, are you blind or just stupid?"

"Nah," said Leery. "What I am is a cop." He flipped out his badge. "And what you are is a Redcap."

"Ain't no law against that! The Grand Cynosure is—"

"Naw," said Ice. "He renounced. Unless you know different?"

The Redcap's shrewd gaze bounced back and forth between them as they spoke, then settled on Dru. "*You* can come in," he said with a leer.

Dru rolled her eyes and chuckled. "Only in your lame dreams," she said.

"What's your name, pal?" asked Leery.

"Noneya."

"Strange name. I expected something like Kleshas Findfault."

"He's up—" The goblin clapped a hand over his mouth, then grimaced and dropped it to his side. "You should be a comedian."

"I get that a lot," said Leery. "How about Comeon Indadoor? Is he inside? Or maybe Howdya Likeacoffee?"

"Qilkwazmerd! Why are you still talking? Close the damn door and be done!"

The goblin snarled. "Cops!" he yelled over his shoulder. A cacophony of footsteps, bottles clinking together, boxes sliding across the floor, and doors slamming sounded upstairs, and a slow smile splashed across the Redcap's face. "Oops."

Leery dropped a heavy hand on his thin shoulder and spun him out into the alley. He pushed up the stairs with a glance over his shoulder. "Tie him up, Ice!" Dru followed Leery up the stairs, taking them two at a time, spinning runes into being with bright flashes of red. Cofy took the Redcap doorman in hand and pressed him face-first into the alley's brick wall.

At the top of the stairs, Leery and Dru burst into a large room, every visible surface painted flat black, even the acoustic ceiling tiles. What looked like a huddle of long-limbed octogenarians sat staring at them through groggy eyes. "Sit right where you are!" Leery yelled, then pointed at a single door in the right corner across the room and dashed toward it. Footsteps pounded overhead, sounding like the Redcaps were herding cattle on the third floor. "I'm going up!"

"Wait for back up, Leery!"

"No time!"

He pounded across Saint Julian's dance floor and flung the door open, raced down the hall, then around and around the spiral staircase leading to the third floor. He erupted into a small square space with two closed doors—one straight ahead and one to his right. He cocked his head a moment, then ran through the right-hand door.

The room beyond was a long rectangle that stretched the length of the building. Bunks lined the inside wall, leaving room for a footlocker and a path along the outside wall.

Goblins in various states of dishabille filled the barracks—some with sleep blindfolds pushed up at strange angles, some staring around bleary-eyed, and others sitting hunched over their own knees as if fighting to keep the vomit in. "Hungover, eh?" Leery cackled as he ran by. Several of the bunks were empty, and he assumed those belonged to the creatures making all that racket running away.

As he approached the other end of the room, one of the Redcaps settled his hat on his head and pushed to his feet, stepping toward the end of his bunk. "What the *fuck* are you—"

Leery stiff-armed the goblin at full speed, sending him flying back into his bunk. "Don't get up!" Leery called. "I can find my own way."

He slammed through the set of double doors at the end of the room and skidded to a halt. Arrayed in front of him were twelve Redcaps, each wearing the same metal-clad boots as the doorman, each with a red cap shoved to some jaunty angle or another, and each holding a murderous-looking iron pike ready, the business ends tracking toward Leery.

"No solicitation!" one of them barked.

"No deliveries before six!" barked another.

"Whoa, whoa, whoa, fellas," said Leery. "I'm a cop."

"About to be a dead cop!" snapped one of the Redcaps.

"Not unless those are silver," Leery said with a grin. "I'm a wolf, you see." He loosened his tie and pulled it off over his head.

The goblin snarled, then barked an order in Ghukliak—the language of goblins, which Leery neither spoke nor could follow in the least—and all twelve of them advanced a stomping step with a sound like the clanking advance of a tank. "Goblins is magic, idiot," said the pikeman.

"Yeah, about that..." Leery unbuttoned his shirt. "See I've fought some of the biggest names in the business. I mean, I went a few rounds with Lucifer, himself, the other week, yet here I am."

Another harsh word in Ghukliak brought the Redcaps a step closer with another crashing lunge. "He ain't no goblin! And you're in *our house* now, fella!"

"No, he's not a gobbo by a long shot," grunted Leery, hopping on one foot while he pulled a Florsheim off. "But few can argue that he's not just brimming with magic. And listen, I'm only looking for a goblin by the name of Findfault. Kleshas Findfault. This doesn't have to get ugly."

Another barking gurgle in Ghukliak, another clanging step, and the twelve Redcaps were almost within striking distance. "With you involved, I bet everything is ugly," said their leader.

"Hey, that's funny. You Findfault, then?" Leery kicked off his other shoe and went to work on his belt, backing a step away to buy more time for his striptease. In the room behind him, he heard more goblins getting organized. "Maybe I should have waited for backup," he grumbled.

"I don't know a Findfault," said the goblin. "I don't know you, neither."

"Oh, I'm sorry. Leery Oriscoe's the name. I'm a cop. Supernatural Inquisitors Squad." He unzipped his pants and shoved them down.

Another harsh command in Ghukliak rattled through the air, and all at once, the twelve Redcaps charged him, their pikes leveled. On the second floor, Dru barked a harsh word and something thumped—*crashed*, more like it—and goblins squealed like pigs.

Leery grinned at the Redcap who'd been giving the orders. "Sure you don't want to come along quietly?"

The Redcap snarled, and Leery stepped from his trousers and allowed his wolf to burst forth, snarling and snapping at the little goblins and their iron blades. He threw his head back and howled, loud enough to rattle the bare bulbs hanging from the ceiling in ancient brass chandeliers. He swiped a taloned hand through the row of pikes with a horrendous crash, then leaped high to land behind the row of advancing Redcaps. He barked a laugh and swept into their midst, flinging small bodies hither and yon.

Out in the alley, Cofy's singsong chanting yielded to a resounding, jangling boom, and Atekhomen rasped his greeting. On the floor beneath his feet, Dru barked in the *Verba Patiendi*, and in front of Leery, the Redcaps regained their feet, reformed, and spun like a military unit, leveling their pikes again.

Leery beckoned at them, his tongue snaking out between his canines and wetting his lupine lips. Then he snarled, dropped to all fours, and launched himself forward, slamming into them at waist level. Five of the goblins went down beneath him, and he thrashed among them, a whirling dervish of taloned sweeps, brutal kicks, and vicious elbows. After half a minute, he spun to his hind legs, dancing back from the porcupine of spears held by the remaining seven.

Another thumping crash vibrated up through the soles of their feet, and the Redcaps still standing straightened a little, looking at one another. The one giving the orders barked something in Ghukliak and swatted the goblin standing next to him with the back of his hand. He pointed at Leery and shoved the man forward while directing two others to see to their fallen friends. Leery rushed forward, a harsh growl rumbling in his chest, and five of the Redcaps snapped their pikes up to meet him.

A lump of gleaming gold began to percolate up through the floor, flowing like water from cracks in the floorboards. It plopped together, a snowman melting in reverse, and once the eidolon's face had formed enough to allow it, Atekhomen hissed, "Detective. My summoner sent me to assist you…if necessary."

Leery sent a lupine grin his way and lunged at the Redcap giving the commands, taking the goblin's iron pike in his mouth and shaking it away, snarling. He bore down, cracking the oak haft of the weapon, then dropped it into his taloned hands and snapped it over his knee.

The Redcap cried out in rage and charged Leery, fists swinging in wide, wild arcs, almost frothing at the mouth. Atekhomen slapped an amorphous blob of an arm out, and the Redcap slammed into it headfirst with a sound like a ringing gong. The Redcap fell in a heap of uncoordinated limbs, eyes rolling, blood from his bitten tongue drooling from the corner of his mouth.

The balance of the Redcaps knotted into a circular formation, standing shoulder to shoulder, and presenting their pikes to all sides. Leery hunched toward them, snarling and snapping his teeth, looking for an opening.

"Stand away, Detective," grated Atekhomen. Without waiting, he snapped his arms out wide, then drove his palms together with a tremendous crash. The Redcaps still on their feet dropped their pikes with a clatter and clapped their hands over their ears. Leery staggered to the wall, ears ringing, half-stunned by the sound.

Atekhomen sped toward the Redcaps, sharp edges and thorn-like protrusions snapping into existence from all parts of his body. A harsh metallic sound issued from the creature's lips and thunder rumbled as

Atekhomen fell among them, limbs blurring, edges growing bright with the heat of scything through the air at blazing speed. The goblins shrieked in pain and terror, climbing over one another in their panic to get away.

Leery shook his head—trying to clear away the harsh ringing buzz—and pushed himself away from the wall, taking a single step toward the whirling sawblade form. He howled and fast-changed back to human form. "Atekhomen! Stop!" he cried, but the eidolon paid him no mind.

The five Redcaps fell in splashes of bloody gore in a wide circle around him, the other Redcaps staring at the eidolon with a kind of horrified awe.

"Atekhomen, *restrain* them, you idiot Cuisinart!"

Without stopping his murderous spin, Atekhomen thrust his head toward Leery and grinned. "My summoner made no demands of me, Detective. I'm free! Free to do as *I* choose!"

Leery shook his head and dashed back to the double doors, still naked as a jaybird. He flung the doors open and shouted, "*ICE!*" Then, he turned back and glared at Atekhomen. "Listen, golden boy, we're the cops. The *good guys*, you know? We don't go around committing mass murder—"

Atekhomen ceased his madcap spinning and gave Leery a bored look. "Oh, *relax*, Detective. I haven't even killed *one* of them." He waved a blade-studded hand at the heap of bleeding Redcaps. "They'll be all right." He glanced down at them. "Probably."

Leery grunted and pointed at one of the worst. "I think his arm's off."

"A mere flesh wound," said Atekhomen with a sniff.

Dru came through the double doors, eyes wide as she took in the destruction Atekhomen had wrought. She turned a blazing-eyed glare on the eidolon. "You've overstepped, protean."

Atekhomen shrugged. "My summoner gave me no constraints except not to kill anyone." He sniffed. "No one is dead."

Dru's eyes narrowed. "Get you gone!" she hissed.

Atekhomen stood, stock-still for a moment, staring back at her, his face as still as if cast in gold, then he nodded and disappeared with a pop.

Ice sprinted in from the barracks room. "SWAT's downstairs. I sent—" He snapped his mouth shut as he caught sight of the Redcaps

Atekhomen had attacked. "I'll kill him," he muttered, hand on his forehead.

18

Lieutenant Van Helsing closed the door to her office, her face an expressionless slab of ectoplasm, though she pulsed in and out of phase almost too quickly to perceive. She glided to her desk, then *through* her desk, then turned to face the group of dour faces across from her. "As I understand it, the eidolon did the damage?"

Leery nodded. "I tried, Lieu, but—"

"Naw. It was my fault. I rushed the summoning, and I wasn't specific enough." Ice frowned. "Atekhomen can be…" He shook his head. "He's a blood-thirsty bastard is what he is, and he's always trying to wriggle out of my constraints when it comes to violence. That's why I usually don't send him off on his own."

Van Helsing sank down in her chair, then sank through it a bit. "And how does Captain Cragrek handle it when your protean goes wild like this?"

Ice shrugged. "I only sent him in because it sounded like all hell was breaking loose inside, and I could see Redcaps getting away across the rooftops. Danny..." Ice shrugged. "Atekhomen hasn't acted out since I've been with SVU."

"And it was twelve to one," said Leery. "And they had iron pikes."

"But you're a werewolf, Leery," murmured Van Helsing. "Iron pikes can't hurt you."

"Yeah, my mother always said the same about names, but no one ever called *her* Fido." Leery flashed a sickly grin. "And besides, they told me themselves that they were *magical* creatures and *could* hurt me if they wanted to."

Epatha sighed and closed her eyes. "Well, we'll deal with what may come when it arrives." She looked at Leery. "You and Dru do the interview. McCoy himself is coming to observe, so watch your p's and q's."

"Right, Lieu," said Leery. "And can you see if we can get Evie over as well. She had court this afternoon, but she should hear this, too."

19

Leery banged into the interview room, holding a couple of mugs of coffee, then spun around to hold the door open for Dru with his foot. She stepped by him and walked around the table, head down, open file folder in front of her. She sat without looking up at the suspect, and Leery came around to sit next to her. "I just love coffee," he said. "How about you Findfault? Do you like your rocket fuel as nature intended it, or do you like to ruin it with a bunch of sugar and crap?"

The goblin across from them—the one who'd been giving the pike crew orders—curled his lip.

"We make a pretty mean cuppa here if you're interested, and I'd be happy to give you a cup." He glanced at the one-way mirror. "No strings attached. I'll give you a cup if you talk to us or not."

"Tell me," mused Dru. "Are you Kleshas or Klignas?"

The goblin sneered but sniffed at Leery's coffee, nonetheless.

"Want a cup? Just say the word."

"Klignas, then," said Dru with a nod. "Where's your brother? Was he one of the men running away across the rooftops?"

"Come on, Klignas. We can *help* you if you'll only help us a little bit. Why'd your crew want an alchemist?"

"You don't know *anything* about what's going on here. Why should I throw in with your lot? Bunch of late-to-the-party types without a clue."

Leery shrugged and put on a wide, wolfish smile. "We caught you, didn't we?"

"You wouldn't have if that...if that...that *Shrike* hadn't shown up!"

"I didn't see a butcherbird back at your nightclub. Did you see one, Dru?"

Klignas scoffed. "Don't you *read*? *Hyperion Cantos*?" He glanced back and forth between them. "Dan Simmons?"

Dru shrugged.

"Benighted, untutored imbeciles!"

"Oh, now our feelings are hurt," snipped Leery.

"Throwing in with you lot would be like filling my own shoes with cement and tossing myself into the sea."

"I'll say it again. We caught you, didn't we? Not bad for a pair of unlearned lowbrows. Don't you think, Dru?"

She leaned forward and rested her forearms on the table, wrists together. "Come on, Klignas," she crooned. "What could it hurt to talk to us? Don't you like me?"

Leery glanced at her and then gulped coffee.

"Oh, stow that alluring elfin tripe," said Klignas. "I'm a *goblin* if you hadn't noticed. All this…this…*flirtation* is insulting."

Dru sighed and sat back, casting a wan smile at Leery. "Can't blame a girl for trying."

The goblin scoffed.

"Why are the Redcaps interested in the Manhattan snack trade?" Leery asked in a hard voice. "Why bother with the gnomes, the leprechauns?"

"That's for me to know, and you to find out," said Klignas. "Now, if you don't mind, I'd like to go back to that travesty of a holding cell and await my magister."

"Are you sure? We could—" A knock sounded on the mirrored glass, and Leery snapped his mouth shut.

"Uh-oh," said Klignas. "Sounds like Master wants you, wolf. Better snap-to. Better heel."

"Right," grumbled Leery.

20

Sam McCoy waited in the observation room, along with Angie, Van Helsing, and Ice. Sam leaned against the far wall, arms laced across his chest, a massive frown on his face. He glanced at them from beneath his wild eyebrows and sucked his teeth. "I don't like it. He's too confident for someone facing the charges we've got him for."

"You think?" asked Leery. "He's got something up his sleeve all right. The question is, what?"

"Maybe he's got a high-dollar magister," said Ice.

Sam shook his head. "Attempted murder of a law enforcement officer, extortion of a public official, assault and battery, resisting arrest, and that's for starters. I'll throw the book at him, and he's got to know that." He clucked his tongue and dropped his gaze to the floor. "No, he's got something bullet-proof."

"What do you want us to do with him?" asked Van Helsing. "We can lose his paperwork until the morning, but…"

Sam grimaced and shook his head. "No. We cut no corners on this one, Epatha. Book him and get him transferred. Then start digging. We have to tie these Redcaps to the Gardeners, the Leprechauns...all the way back to Raguel."

A knock on the outer door sounded, and Leery opened it. Puriel stood outside, a small grin on his face. "I can help with that," he said. "And more."

"I'm all ears," said Sam, lifting his busy eyebrows.

Puriel stepped through the door and closed it behind him. "Dawn and I have been doing some rooting around."

"Where is she, anyway?" asked Ice.

"She had to get back to the Thirteenth," Puriel said. "Raguel was a troubled soul," he said. "Very close to falling, which is troublesome for the angel tasked to watch her brothers and sisters and keep them on the straight and narrow. But she was very bored with her calling."

"Bored?" asked Ice. "How does an angel get bored?"

He sighed. "Consider eternity, Detective Cofy. Plus, there's the archangel factor."

"The archangel factor?"

"Yes. They get all the press, get the fancy flaming swords, are seen in His presence often, that kind of thing."

"You mean..." Leery shook his head. "You angels get *jealous* of one another?"

Puriel lifted his shoulders. "It's a temptation for everyone, is it not?"

"Raguel was bored and tired of her job," said McCoy. "How does that tie all this together?"

"Her dissatisfaction has grown for a few centuries—and her visits to Gehenna did little to help her." He cast a baleful eye at Dru. "We had expected her to be repulsed, but..."

"Sorry to disappoint," Dru said with a sneer.

"You are forgiven," said Puriel in a lofty tone. "Raguel sought...*flavor*. She sought novel experiences, anything to make her feel better, no matter how transient feelings derived in that way may be. I spoke with her about it on several occasions." He shrugged. "I failed to impress, I suppose."

"When do we get to the part where this circus starts to make sense," said Leery.

"Raguel began to abuse snacks some time ago, but recently, she'd gone through rehab and seemed to be back to her usual self." Puriel frowned. "Dawn and I checked her domicile, however, and found it in quite a state." He wrinkled his nose. "She had debts, you see."

McCoy lifted an eyebrow. "Debts big enough to get her killed?"

"So it seems," said Puriel. "She owed a tidy sum to the Gardeners for her past snack habit. And she owed the Unknown—the Redcaps."

"Wait a minute," said Leery. "The Unknown are trying to break into the snack business. How could she have run up a tab if they—"

"Gambling, Detective. Among other things."

"But you can't collect from a dead person," said Ice. "Everyone knows that."

Puriel shrugged. "The Redcaps also bought her debts from the gnomes."

Leery's eyes narrowed. "That's strange."

"Yes," said Puriel.

"So Raguel runs up debts for various vices. The Redcaps buy her debts from the lesser organizations, and they, in turn, help twist up the investigation into her murder." Sam shook his head and raised his hands out to the sides. "Why?"

"Our best bet for answering that question just invoked his rights," said Leery with a frown.

"Then we'll just have to answer the questions ourselves," said Sam in an exasperated tone.

Chapter 3

The Court Case

I

Sam frowned at the folder spread open on his desk. He drew a deep breath and puffed out his cheeks, glancing at Angie from beneath his wrinkled brow. He reached out and flipped the folder closed. "Thin."

Angie grimaced and slid the folder from his desk. "I know, but it's all we have so far."

Sam shook his head. "Puriel contends that she owed money all over town and that the Redcaps bought it all. Detective Evans and CBI OC squad tell us that the Redcaps have increased their spending by a factor of five, but they can't trace the source of the funds. So far. They can't say *why* the Redcaps are spending so heavily, either, but they're still digging."

"I know," said Angie in a quiet voice.

"If you'll pardon the terrible pun, that's a lot of unknowns to go to trial with."

Carmichael flashed a one-sided grin. "That *is* terrible."

"Glad you enjoyed it. What do we do about it?"

"We could take another run at some of the lesser actors. Maybe flip our way to the top."

Sam leaned back in his chair and grimaced down at his hands. "So far, the suspects we have in custody are one of two types: low-level types, and high-level types with excellent magisters who've been coached to invoke the second we get them in the box." He sighed. "Have you heard who Findfault's being represented by?"

Angie shook her head.

"Dworkin. Know who the Gardener captains have? Shatenstein."

Carmichael's frown was back. "All we need to have the perfect defense team is Tovah."

Sam grimaced and spun his chair so he could look out the window.

"No…"

"Yes," murmured Sam. "She's representing Muircheartach Mac Cárthaigh, and she's already moved for the trials to be joined."

Angie pinched the bridge of her nose. "Maybe we should just decline to prosecute."

"Perish the thought," said Sam with some of his normal vigor. "But we need bullets for our six-guns, Angie. And we need the hard calibers, no suppositions, no maybes."

Angie sighed and switched to rub her temples. "I'm getting a headache."

"Better stock up on the aspirin, then, because this mess is just getting started."

2

Leery hustled from the coffee machine, his ears filled with the shrieking of the ringer Dru had installed on his cell phone the last time he'd made her send a text for him. The damn thing lay on the blotter of his desk, right next to the landline phone, where all phones should be if you asked him. He flashed an uneasy smile at the other detectives in the squad room, not really sure why they thought the song she'd used as his ringer was so funny.

The song rolled into the chorus and the room rolled into laughter, even though the lyrics didn't seem to be funny. *Never gonna give you up, never gonna let you down,* he thought. *What's funny about that?* He forced a chuckle as though he got the joke, then swept the phone up and smashed his thumb against its screen until the ringing stopped. He pressed the phone to his ear. "Oriscoe," he said, and the other detectives broke into applause. Leery waved his hand and sank into his chair.

"Hey, Wonder Dog," said Evie. "How's tricks?"

"Great, great, Evie. If you count being neck-deep in DD-9s."

"You never were any good at paperwork."

"What are you talking about, *Yvonne*? All of my paperwork was always on time and always top-notch when I worked with you."

"That's because *I did it all*, you bozo. Speaking of which, where's your partner?"

Leery glanced around the squad room. "Dunno. She was here a minute ago. What's up?"

"I've got something for you, but no one's going to like it."

"Well, gee, Evie, that sounds just wonderful. Thanks for calling to ruin my life."

"Oh, it's my pleasure, Leery."

He put down his cup of coffee and pulled a pad from Dru's desk, then reached back and stole a pen. "Shoot."

"That didn't take you long. She must not be hiding the pens, yet."

"Nah, she still thinks she's losing them in the car."

"The forensic accountants have been tracing the money like you asked."

"Hey, don't blame me. It's those damn magisters."

"Right. Well, anyway, one of them is kind of a conspiracy nut."

"He's an *accountant*, Evie. You don't have to say the part about being a nut. It's implied."

"*Anyway*," she said. "The Redcap spending increases seem to mirror certain events during the last election, and since."

"Nobody's that stupid, Evie. This guy must be a crackpot."

"It's a she, and she is a crackpot, but this time she's right. I've seen the spreadsheets myself. Someone from the GC's campaign has been diverting funds into a special account for, get this, *catering*, and that account is being drained on a regular basis by…"

"The Unknown."

"Bingo!"

"Oh, not that again. Come on, Evie, the dog thing is getting old."

Silence ticked on the line for a moment, then Evie broke out into braying laughter. "Oh my, Oriscoe, you sound so pathetic."

"Yeah, yeah. Dru put some pop song from the eighties on my phone and now—"

"Oh, my sweet lord! *She rickrolled you?*"

"What? No, it's that song... *Never Gonna Give You Up.*"

"She knows, Oriscoe," said Evie between burst of guffaws. "About the pens, I'll give you odds she knows. That song is by Rick Astley, and it used to be a thing on the internet to get someone to click a link that took them to that song."

"I don't get it."

"You wouldn't. Anyway, I meant bingo as in the thing you yell when you fill your card in a bingo game."

"Well, it's also the name of a dog, so…"

"You really need to get out more, Oriscoe."

Leery sighed. "Yeah, but there are these DD-9s."

Evie chuckled. "Nice try. You want to tell Carmichael so you can steal all the credit for the forensic accountants?"

"It's only fair," he said. "I *did* tell you to use them, after all."

3

Sam slapped a hand over his eyes when Angie relayed the news to him. Acid burbled from his stomach into his throat and began to party, and he frowned sourly. "I need a raise," he mumbled.

"You and me, both, Sam," said Angie. "What do we do?"

McCoy got to his feet. "This decision is above my pay grade. Come on." He led her out the side door of his office and across the hall to Adam's. "Hey, Adam. Got a minute?"

The old magister looked up from a sheaf of papers on his desk and waved them in. "By the looks on your faces, I'd better break out the Glenlivet." Crystal tinkled as he added ice and then scotch to the glasses. He joined the others already sitting across the room on the couch and passed the tumblers of scotch around. "Now, tell me what apocalyptic thing you've discovered."

"We're prepping for the Findfault trial." Sam took a long sip from his tumbler and closed his eyes as the cinnamon and nutty flavor rushed across his palate.

Adam nodded and waved his scotch in a tiny circle, making the ice dance and jingle against the crystal sides of the tumbler.

"Up until now, the link between Raguel and the Redcaps has been tenuous, at best," said Angie. "I mean, we know they bought her debts, but no one seemed to know why."

"I take it you've found something that firms that linkage up?" asked Adam with the tiniest bit of impatience creeping into his voice.

Angie nodded and glanced at Sam.

"Yes," he said. "There is evidence that implicates the new Grand Cynosure."

"What?" hissed Adam, leaning forward in his chair. "Direct evidence?"

Sam shrugged. "Someone in his campaign has been diverting funds to a Redcap organization. The Unknown. Findfault is a part of that organization."

Adam collapsed back in the chair, staring down at his drink. He lifted the tumbler to his lips and polished off his drink in one big gulp. "And how solid is the evidence?"

"The forensic accountancy team for the OC squad dug it up," said Angie. "So, I imagine it's solid, though dryer than the Mojave."

Adam frowned down at his empty glass, then got up and refilled it. "Anyone else ready?" he murmured over his shoulder. When no one answered, he rejoined them, sinking into an easy chair with a sigh. "What do you need?"

Angie glanced at Sam, and the EALM grunted. "We need to know what you want us to do. As I see it, there are a few options. First, we can use the information at trial, thus putting it in the public record. After the trial, we could either drop a dime anonymously or just walk away, letting justice take its course. Second, we could dig deeper, involving the CBI and whoever else we can think of, and split the scam wide open for all and sundry to see. The publicity alone almost guarantees us convictions against the Redcaps and other gangs. Third..." Sam shook his head.

"Third, you ignore it all and go to trial with what you have," said Adam, and Sam nodded. "That's quite the knot you'd like me to untie for you, Sam. In the first option, you get your conviction, but by avoiding the *real* heart of the issue, no?"

Sam nodded.

"Secondly, you might split the Covenancy apart, and at the very least might make the three of us into political pariahs. And if you're wrong..." He shook his head.

Sam glanced at Angie, and they both sipped their drinks.

"And the third option"—Adam shook his head and sneered—"is the coward's way." He drank his scotch, his mouth working, shuttling the amber liquid back and forth over his tongue. "But, at the end of the day, I was elected to represent the people of this locus, to ensure they get justice, and the matter of the greater country, while important, has no bearing here. The third option is out. It leaves you with the weakest case against a criminal organization famous for wiggling out of convictions. So, the real question is this: how does this office wish to be perceived with respect to the possible criminal activities of a sitting Grand Cynosure?"

Sam grimaced and nodded. "That's how I see it."

"Then the knot tends toward the Gordian variety, and so does the solution. Take the second option. As long as I'm seated in the big chair, this office acts in the interests of justice, for the people of the Locus of New York, *and* beyond."

"You're the chief, Chief."

"Right you are, Sam." Adam swirled his scotch, then downed it in two swallows. "You get the job done. I'll take the heat. But you'll be standing next to me later this afternoon."

Sam quirked his eyebrow.

"At the press conference," said Adam. "Try to get someone from the Covenancy there, too."

"I know just the man," said Sam, glancing at Angie.

4

Four hours later, Adam followed Locus Cynosure Endymion up to the podium in the marble foyer of the Locus Magister's office amidst the fluttering cacophony of photographers, camera operators, and journalists. Sam came next, followed by Verbius, then Angie, then Chief Magnussen, Lieutenant Van Helsing, Leery, and Dru.

Endymion rested one hand on the podium, tapped the microphone with the other, then held it up for silence. "Thank you all for coming," he said. "I have a brief statement, which will be followed by the comments of the Locus Magister, Adam Hill. He will answer your questions afterward." He glanced back at Adam, and the LM nodded. "This is a strange time in the Covenancy," began Endymion. "A time when the most convenient answer often seems to be the best, when corners are cut without much comment by the press, the citizenry, or, woefully, the government itself. Many times, this expediency seems the only solution available, but it only appears that way. It is my duty, as the Cynosure of this great locus, to stand up for the right way of doing things, to *lead* by both example and by action. Today, my task, though grim, is to stand by the Locus Magister in his quest for justice. A quest that may take us as far as those gilded halls below the Capitol Building in Washington D.C." He gave them a terse nod, then stepped back. "I give you Adam Hill, Locus Magister."

Adam stepped forward in a silence so perfect that Leery expected the sound of a pin dropping at any moment. "Thank you, Cynosure," he said, nodding to Endymion. "Ladies and gentlemen of the press, during the course of a simple murder investigation, the Supernatural Inquisitors Unit, along with the Occult Cabal Unit, have uncovered evidence that potentially links murder and wanton destruction on a terroristic scale, plots against public officials, extortion, snack running, and more, to individuals close to Grand Cynosure Fidonk Slypinch, if not the Grand Cynosure himself. As we all know, GC Slypinch was once a self-declared Redcap—though, according to his campaign, it was decades ago, and he has since severed all ties with the group. We have developed evidence that the GC may not be so removed from the group as he would have us believe." The journalists all began talking at once, shouting questions, demanding clarification. Adam held up both hands. "Calm, ladies and gentlemen. I will answer your questions at the end of my statement, but we must remain calm." He waited a moment, gazing at them, the picture of serenity, until they quieted. "We have widened our investigation beyond the boundaries of this locus, and as such, we have enjoined the Covenancy Magister for the Southern District of New York to assist us, to lend us aid where barriers such as jurisdiction hamper our efforts. Along with his own significant talent and knowledge, Verbius also brings access to Covenancy agencies such as the CBI and the Covenancy Marshals Service. Now, our investigation into the possible ties to the GC's campaign is just beginning, but our prosecution of the thugs and bad actors within the Locus of New York is already in process, and my own Executive Assistant Locus Magister, Sam McCoy, spearheads that effort. It will proceed apace, and we expect many interesting tidbits will emerge during the trial, including the possibility of eyewitness testimony regarding the involvement of the GC or his campaign. We all hope these concerns come to nothing, as appearances *can* be misleading, but I want to assure the people of this locus, that I will pursue criminal activity to those ultimately responsible for that activity, no matter where that pursuit leads my office. I have only one mandate in mind: to fight for the people of this great locus and to deliver them justice. Thank you." Adam sipped from a bottle of water from behind the podium. "I will now take a few questions."

The room erupted as though someone had tossed in a grenade. Journalists stood, shouted questions, waved their hands, and jostled one another for a clear view of the LM.

"One at a time, please," said Adam with a faint smile on his lips. "Agatha? Your question?"

An older woman smiled at him as the other journalists sat with yet more clatter and confusion. "Thank you, Mr. Hill. My question is this: during the recent campaign season, many journalists wondered about the GC's claims that he had cut all ties with any Redcap organizations he may have once supported—indeed, there were even allegations that some Redcap groups were hired to provide security at some of his rallies—does your evidence point to the *active* interference of the electoral process by Redcap organizations?"

"No, not at this time," said Adam. "Our case concerns activities that have occurred within the last week, though some of the evidence recently developed may lead back to the time of the campaign itself."

"Mr. Hill!" shouted a skinny troll with grayish-green skin and slab-like features. "Mr. Hill, the current case—I understand it began as part of the GC's so-called war on snacks?"

"I can't comment on the details of the case until after the trial," said Adam. "I will say, however, that the defendants in the case were involved with the snack trade."

"Would the Covenancy Magister care to comment on the breadth of the investigation?"

asked a young witch with bright red hair and pale, pale skin.

Adam held up his hand. "Verbius is here at my request, to illustrate our cooperative efforts. He is not yet ready to comment publicly."

Verbius nodded, then started and reached inside his coat and withdrew his cell phone as it began to trill. He glanced down at the screen and paled a little. He raised his gaze to Adam and jerked his chin toward the door.

"That's all, ladies and gentlemen," said Adam, his gaze locked on Verbius' retreating form as he stepped away from the podium and left the lobby via the door through which they'd all entered. "Thank you for coming. Please feel free to submit any additional questions in writing to my office, and we will respond, as always."

The journalists all began shouting questions and leaning forward, waving their hands, their digital records, their pads, or pens.

Adam smiled and waved. As Leery turned to go, his phone began to ring, blaring its silly tune, and Dru snickered. "Very funny," he said around a grin.

5

Verbius stood in the hall, his cell phone plastered to his ear, his gaze on the floor tiles, high color on his cheeks. He looked at them as they filed in and held up his index finger. "Yes, sir," he said and hung up, grimacing. "That was the Magister General."

"I'll talk to him," said Adam.

"He's most upset."

"I'll talk to him."

"He's instructed me to copy everything you've given me and send it to him. He wants me to report everything you do or say to him personally."

"You can't do that," said Sam.

Adam lifted his chin, then lowered it. "I'll talk to him. In the meantime, we have a case to prosecute and an investigation to kick off. Let's get to it."

They split up, and Sam led Angie back upstairs and into his office. "Want to write me another brilliant opening?" he said over his shoulder.

She grinned. "Sure. It's kind of fun."

"You won't feel the same way in five more years."

"Have you decided on the charges?"

"For Muircheartach Mac Cárthaigh, it's easy. Twenty-three counts of magical murder in the first degree, fraud, magical obfuscation of justice, four counts of assault and battery on law enforcement officers, seventeen counts of assault and battery against individuals, and giving a false statement with the intent to mislead an ongoing investigation."

"I have a feeling that last one is going to be popular."

Sam nodded. "Definitely. Both Jenkor and Reknad get one count each. In addition, they each get three counts of assault and battery against law enforcement officers." He shook his head. "But none of that matters until we beat Tovah's joinder motion."

"That may be tough, given the press conference we've just been part of," said Angie.

"I know, but you'll find a way. You always do."

Angie rolled her eyes. "A little guidance from time to time would make it easier. But what about Klignas Findfault and his little band of pikemen?"

"I think we'll go with the attempted murder of a law enforcement officer and resisting."

"What about the extortion of Alentina Washburn? What about the Raguel murder?"

Sam bunched his eyebrows and tapped his chin with his forefinger. "For now, we'll hold those charges. If we win the hearing on joining the cases, we can reconsider it."

"Well, even if we win, you know the second you add those charges, Tovah will refile the motion."

"Ah, but once the matter is decided for her client, she has no standing in what we do against Findfault."

Angie smiled. "That's tricksy, Sam. I hadn't considered that."

"Hopefully, neither has Tovah."

6

Bailiff Thoridn stepped forward and struck his halberd against the floorboards with a resounding thump. "Order! Order! All rise and give respect to Her Honor, the Just Grimhildr Gyuki!"

Sam and Angie stood, and Thoridn treated them to a nod dressed up with a severe expression. Gyuki charged into the courtroom, her black silk robes snapping in the wind of her passage. She took up her gavel, nodded at Sam, then turned her placid blue eyes on the defense magisters. "It hardly seems fair," she said. "Three of you against the LM's office." She banged her gavel without waiting for a reply, settled into her chair, and turned to Thoridn. "Thank you, dear one." He ducked his head, tugging his forelock, then stepped back to his place. "I have the motion filed by Ms. Melnick, Mr. Dworkin, and Mr. Shatenstein here in front of me. I call this session to order to decide its merits. Ms. Melnick, would you care to begin?"

"Thank you, Your Honor," said Tovah, rising to her feet. "Though it doesn't impact our legal arguments, I would like to draw the Court's attention to the press conference held by the Locus Cynosure and Locus Magister two days ago."

"I saw it," said Gyuki.

"In light of that press conference, I find myself wondering if there is any need for a hearing on this matter? The Locus Magister himself seems convinced that the—"

Sam lurched to his feet. "Your Honor—"

"Nice try, Ms. Melnick," said Gyuki holding up a hand for silence. "But I think we'll rely on legal arguments to decide the matter." She lowered her hand and turned a cold expression on the defense magister. "Do you have any?"

"Uh, yes, Your Honor. The prosecution's theory of the case is that my client acted in furtherance of a crime perpetrated by members of the Gardeners, a street gang of gnomes located in the East Village. It seems—"

"Forgive me, I must be getting old." Gyuki's sparkling eyes and sly expression gave lie to the statement. "I don't see where your client is charged with conspiracy?"

"Well, no, Your Honor, but—"

"Then how do you support your motion that the two distinct lists of charges should, in fact, be joined? If the prosecution hasn't found evidence of a conspiracy, then—"

"Begging your pardon, Your Honor, but the prosecution has such evidence in spades. My client's statement provides—"

"And the statement you refer to is the alleged false statement for which the prosecutor *has* levied charges against your client?"

Tovah grimaced. "Yes, Judge. But—"

"Then are these four counts of assault and battery on law enforcement officers the same crime as that the Gardeners are charged with?"

"No, Your Honor."

"Hmm. I see that the Gardeners are also charged with giving a false statement?" She turned her gaze on Sam.

"Yes, Your Honor," said Sam. "Jenkor the Rake and Reknad the Machete both pointed fingers at the Leprechaun gang, and Reknad even named Ms. Melnick's client, but with regard to crimes separate to what we've charged Muircheartach Mac Cárthaigh with."

"One feels the need for a street map…" murmured Grimhildr. "Ms. Melnick, I fail to see anything supporting your motion. Mr. Dworkin, it hardly seems a good use of the Court's time to allow arguments as to your client, judging from the charges levied."

Dworkin stood and cleared his throat. "Your Honor, if I might point out, the three cases, though they appear to be separate crimes, are, in fact, in furtherance of a larger crime. The crimes alleged by the Locus Magister in his press conference, in fact. Each of us"—he swept his hand to encompass Shatenstein and

Melnick—"represent clients whose actions were driven by an overarching goal."

Gyuki held up her hand. "Before you go on, Mr. Dworkin, I'd like to remind you that your statements before the Court are a matter of public record. Do you assert that the conspiracy alleged by the Locus Magister does, in fact, exist? Do you concede that the Grand Cynosure, or someone within his campaign organization, joined in concert with your clients, in an act to defraud the citizens of the Covenancy?" The courtroom took on a funereal silence as Gyuki glared at each defense magister in turn. "If any of you would like to stipulate such, I'd be happy to consider the matter." Again, Grimhildr's gaze swept across them, though none of them returned it.

"I withdraw my previous statements, Your Honor. I spoke in haste," said Dworkin.

"Ah, I see. In that case, can we dispense with this argument?"

Shatenstein stood and glanced at McCoy. "Your Honor, we feel that it is only a matter of time until Mr. McCoy charges our clients with the conspiracy."

"Oh?" Gyuki arched a fine eyebrow. "And has our system of justice descended so far as to allow the feelings of defense magisters in lieu of evidence?"

Shatenstein grimaced.

"Because, Mr. Shatenstein, I see no evidence. I see little in the way of valid legal arguments, given the current charges."

"Then perhaps we can table the motion for such future time as the LM's office does levy charges of conspiracy?"

Grimhildr sat back in her chair, head cocked to the side, and stared at Shatenstein for a few moments. "Perhaps." She turned her gaze on Sam. "What about it, Mr. McCoy?"

"Your Honor, the point is moot."

Gyuki arched her eyebrow.

"These charges will never be eligible for joining, Your Honor, regardless of other things the defendants may be charged with in the future. Those hypothetical future charges would require a motion on merit of their own in order to join the trials."

The judge sat back, pursed her lips, and stared at nothing. "It occurs to me that the joining of the charges brought in these three trials offers undue advantage to the defense."

"But, Your Honor—"

Gyuki held up her hand. "No, Mr. Dworkin, it's my turn, now. The advantage gained by the defense is that the prosecution must, by definition, prove charges that are not levied against the defendants, to wit, that all three cases are linked by an overarching conspiracy of criminal activity, and that each of these unrelated charges must be in furtherance of that conspiracy." She shrugged. "Frankly, Mr. McCoy has pressed charges against your clients that are unrelated, except by the alleged conspiracy. Your motion is denied." Gyuki rapped her gavel and nodded to McCoy.

"Thank you, Your Honor," he said with a slight bow.

"Court dismissed." She flashed a smile at him, then whirled around and left the chamber, gliding across the floor as if on invisible wings. Thoridn rapped his halberd on the floor, then turned smartly to his right and left the room.

Sam turned to Angie and smiled. "I told you you'd figure out the right argument to make."

She smiled a little. "Too bad you never got a chance to use it."

"I'll save it for the next joinder motion."

7

Tovah knocked on the doorjamb, then came in through the open door before Sam had a chance to invite her in. She smiled at Angie and put her valise on the table attached at right angles to Sam's desk. "Got a minute?" she asked.

"I thought you might come by this afternoon," said Sam.

"Should I step out?" asked Angie.

"No, this visit is all business," said Tovah with a grin and a wink at Sam. "I've come to broach the subject of a plea agreement."

Sam's bushy eyebrows went up, and a faint smile brushed his lips. "One of the things I've always admired about you, Tovah, is your brashness."

"Thank you…I think." She slid a chair out across from Angie and sat. "Well? Is there wiggle room regarding my client's charges?"

"Muircheartach Mac Cárthaigh killed twenty-three gnomes in Tompkins Square Park," said Angie. "Plus injuring seventeen more and attacking four cops."

"And one angel," added Sam.

"Yes," said Tovah. "And he needs to pay for those crimes. I'm not so brash as to expect him to walk."

Sam shook his head. "What information could he possibly be a party to that would mitigate any of his just punishment?"

Tovah fought to suppress a grin. "What if he has information into the conspiracy you're tiptoeing around?"

Sam glanced at Angie. "I can't imagine he knows much that Adam would be interested in."

"You might be surprised. Mack is one of the founders of the Leprechauns, remember. His actions in the park—his *confession* to his actions—represent a big sacrifice that came with a big reward for the gang. The Redcaps made certain promises that were unbelievable without other supporting evidence."

"Evidence? Or hearsay?" asked Angie.

"Well, that's up to the judge, but I can think of at least two exceptions to the hearsay rule."

"And you'll argue them on our behalf?"

"I have to draw the line at making your case for you. You'll still have to do the prosecution yourselves."

"Let's hear it," said Sam.

"First, let's discuss the terms."

Sam squinted at her for a moment, then stood and went across the hall. When he returned, Adam Hill was behind him.

Adam nodded at Tovah. "Ms. Melnick."

"Mr. Hill. Good to see you again. How is your lovely wife?"

"Doing well, thank you for asking. Sam tells me you want to make our case."

"My client does, actually. In exchange for consideration."

Adam sighed. "A mass murderer wants leniency?"

"He knows he's going to the dungeons, but he needs protection. He knows too much, and that, on top of the nature of his crimes, paints a bright target on his back."

Adam pursed his lips. "How many murder counts?" he asked Sam.

"Twenty-three."

The Locus Magister sucked his teeth. "That's a lot of blood, Tovah. I'll need a preview of his information before I decide."

Tovah frowned. "I suppose it can't be avoided."

"No," said Adam firmly. "It cannot." He sat down to listen, and his expression grew darker and darker the more she told him.

8

Five days later, Leery and Dru stepped off a train in Grand Central Station, a gray-faced goblin in handcuffs between them. Sam McCoy waited on the platform, and he grinned at Leery. "Good trip?"

"Sure, if you like constant complaining, frequent trips to the bathroom, and foul stenches. Meet Ivtavin Wildeye"—he pushed the goblin forward by the shoulder—"His Grace the Grand Cynosure's former campaign manager. Say hello to your doom, Ivtavin—Sam the Stakeman McCoy."

Ivtavin grumbled something under his breath.

Sam looked him up and down, a fierce frown settling on his features. "I'm on lunch break from court, but I hope—for your sake—you are prepared to talk to me afterward." Ivtavin did nothing but sneer, and McCoy sighed. "You can lead a horse to water…"

"But you can't hit him with a phonebook," said Leery.

"You've read him his rights?" asked Sam.

"In front of a whack of reporters, and live on Covenancy Watch Television," said Dru. "I think it's documented."

"In a case with as broad of implications as this, it had better be." Sam half-turned, then cocked his head at the goblin. "Well, Wildeye? What's it to be? Do we book you into the system and cart you out to Rikers Island, or do we get you a suite at the Plaza? I've got to get back, so I have no time for screwing around."

"I won't be talking to you without the aid of my magister," said Wildeye. "He'll be up by this evening."

"Ah," said Sam. He switched his gaze to Leery. "Book him. When his magister is ready to talk, they can call my office for an appointment."

"Right," said Leery. He tightened his grip on the goblin's thin arm. "Hear that, Wildeye? You get to go to Rikers with all the criminals. I bet they have a special shiv already picked out for you."

"Rikers?" asked the goblin. "I assumed…"

"What? That we'd take you out for lunch? Nah. We save that for cooperative—"

"Book him, Detective," said Sam. "Unless he'd rather go to the Two-Seven's interrogation room? I can get you a defense magister until yours arrives."

Ivtavin glanced around as though there was someone nearby to tell him what to do. "No thank you on the public defender, but please don't book me," he whined. "If you let me make a local call, I can speed Mr. Blighttongue up."

Leery arched an eyebrow at McCoy, who said, "From the precinct. Make sure he gets his phone call, Detective." He gave Leery a look, then turned to go. "You can book him after supper if his magister doesn't arrive. Meanwhile, I'm due back in court."

"Will do," said Leery, a small, crafty smile on his lips. "And McCoy? Nail those gnomes to the wall, will ya?"

9

Later that afternoon, a goblin in a five-thousand-dollar suit stepped into the Supernatural Inquisitors squad room and wrinkled his nose. He held a calfskin attaché case in one hand and his cell phone in the other.

Leery glanced down at his cell phone and grinned. "Well, you certainly took your sweet time," he said.

The goblin turned his all-black gaze on Leery and sneered. "You must be Detective Oriscoe."

"Aw, what gave it away? The fact that I'm not a woman or the lack of horns?"

"The smell, sir. The smell."

"Hey, I showered yesterday, and I use Axe body wash, so if there's a smell, better check your shoes."

The goblin sneered. "My client?"

"What's your name, pal?"

"Fizhauk Blighttongue."

"Great name for a magister," Leery mumbled. "The interrogation room's through that door. I'll bring Wildeye in." He glanced at the holding cell and the goblin with glistening, mournful eyes who stood at the barred door.

"And this McCoy? Is he here, too?"

Leery shrugged. "Nah. I'll give him a call and see if he can make it."

"*If* he can make it?"

Leery grinned. "Hey, in this locus, we work for a living, and *he's* not the one that took five hours to show up."

Wildeye whimpered, and Blighttongue rolled his eyes and turned toward the interrogation room. "Bring my client!" the magister snapped. "At once!"

"Hey, relax. I'm getting to it," said Leery, putting his feet up on his desk and dialing Dru on his cell phone. "Dru? Yeah, the mouthpiece is here." He grinned and gave Blighttongue a little wave. "Right. I'll give Sam a call." He thumbed the disconnect button.

Blighttongue stood staring at him through narrowed eyelids.

"Help you with something else?" Leery asked. "If not..." He made a shooing gesture toward the interrogation room. In a huff, the magister sneered, spun on his heel, and slammed through the interrogation room door, while Leery grinned. He dialed Sam and leaned back in his chair. "Hey, Sam. He's here."

"Took his sweet time, didn't he?" Sam said.

"Yeah, but it's okay, he brought his attitude with him."

"He asked for me?"

"Second thing he asked me for, the first being his client."

"Right. I bet it will take you fifteen minutes to clear your desk before you can accommodate him."

"Hey, it could take up to an hour. I'm very messy," said Leery looking at his empty desktop. "You know how hard I work."

"Right, right. But I think fifteen minutes will be enough. Did Wildeye make his call?"

"He sure did."

"Local?"

"Yep. To—and you're going to love this—a certain heavy metal club in Brooklyn. The guy who answered the phone called himself Kleshas."

"Ah, the elusive Kleshas Findfault."

"Right. Our friend Kleshas then connected Wildeye to a law firm in D.C."

"And he stayed on the line."

"You bet. I've got the whole thing recorded for you. Dru dropped it with Angie a couple hours ago."

"Excellent. I'll listen to it on my way over."

10

Dru smiled as she entered the observation room and handed Leery a *trenta* cup of coffee from Starbucks. She passed out talls to both Sam and Angie, then nodded to Van Helsing. "Hello, Lieu." She held out the last tall cup. "Would you like a coffee?"

Epatha snorted. "Thanks, but before you bring me a cuppa, better bring a mop as well. My middle-piece leaks like a sieve these days. I do appreciate the thought, though."

Dru dimpled and sipped from the cup. "Did I miss anything?"

"No, we're just waiting—"

Blighttongue got up and knocked on the window.

"—for that, I guess," said Angie.

Sam led Angie into the interrogation room, wearing a severe frown. "ALM Sam McCoy, and this is ALM Angie Carmichael."

"Fizhauk Blighttongue, of Blighttongue, Brightflame, and Grumpneck. I take it you already know my client."

Sam pulled out a chair for Angie, then sat next to her. "My time is valuable, Blighttongue, and we're here at your request."

"Straight to business. Good. I like that," said Blighttongue. "My client wishes to cooperate fully with your prosecution."

Sam arched his eyebrow. "Is that so?" He glanced at Ivtavin Wildeye.

"Indeed, he does. Further, Mr. Wildeye is prepared to make a full confession and throw himself on the mercy of the court."

"In return for? I hope you understand that we will require testimony in exchange for any deal." He quirked an eyebrow. "And, I should mention we already have all the evidence we need to sink your client." He pulled a digital recorder out of his coat pocket. "Everything he discussed with you earlier today."

Blighttongue grinned. "Magister-client privilege—"

"Doesn't apply when there's a third party on the phone," said Angie. "And there's that recording at beginning of Wildeye's call that made it all explicit the call would be recorded and may be used against him."

The magister turned a hostile glare on his client. "You let Findfault stay on the line?" he hissed, and Wildeye hung his head.

"I didn't..."

Blighttongue cursed, then forced himself to smile and nod at McCoy. "Well, played, Mr. McCoy, but that changes nothing. My client still wishes to cooperate. He'll just have to serve his time."

"Let me get this straight," said Angie. "Wildeye here wants to fall on his sword, even though he'll get no consideration, no deal, and no plea agreement?"

The defense magister's grin faltered, and he ducked his gaze away from hers. "That *is* what I said."

Angie glanced at Sam, but he focused his attention on Wildeye. "Why would you do that?" he asked.

Looking glum, Wildeye glanced at his magister from the corner of his eye and shrugged.

"We haven't discussed the potential charges yet, and I'm not prepared to do so at this time, but sentencing could be severe—ranging from decades to multiple lifetimes depending on where your confession takes us. Why wouldn't you at least want a trial?"

"You may address yourself to me, sir," said Blighttongue, lifting his chin and glaring at Sam.

"I'll address myself to whomever I damn-well please!" snapped Sam. "And right now, I want to speak to your client."

"Don't answer him," said Blighttongue.

Again, Wildeye looked at his magister askance, then slumped deeper into his chair.

Sam narrowed his eyes and turned his attention on Blighttongue. "I wonder who else Blighttongue, Brightflame, and Grumpneck represent? Politicians?"

The magister in his fancy suit flashed a lopsided grin across the table and folded his arms. "It seems to me that my client list is none of your business."

Sam shrugged. "Maybe not, but it's certainly something your client might be interested in. For instance, if you represented another goblin new to the District of Columbia."

"Hmph. I represent many goblins in many different cities."

"And I imagine more than a few in the government of this great Covenancy," said Angie. "Staffers, civil servants... Grand Cynosures?"

Blighttongue spared her a scathing glance and curled his lip. "If you are suggesting that I represent His Excellency the Grand

Cynosure, allow me to set your small minds at ease, as I do not."

"But perhaps one of your partners does?" asked McCoy, with a significant glance at Wildeye.

"That is neither here nor there," said the magister. "*I* represent Mr. Wildeye, not my partners."

"Uh-huh," said Sam. He switched his gaze to Wildeye and leaned across the table toward him. "I can have one of the best defense magisters in the City here within the hour. I strongly suggest you consider retaining unbiased representation before you make any binding mistakes."

Blighttongue shook his head. "Do you wish to take his confession or don't you? Because if you do not, I see no reason to sit here and be insulted."

"Maybe..." murmured Wildeye sitting up straight.

"*Wildeye!*" snapped Blighttongue. "Remember your commitments."

Ivtavin slumped back and sighed. He dropped his gaze to his hands. "Yes, of course," he murmured.

Sam's narrow-eyed gaze darted back and forth between the two goblins for a moment. "Mr. Wildeye?"

"No…Mr. Blighttongue speaks for me," he whispered.

McCoy shook his head and gave his teeth a suck. "This is a mistake. Surely you see that you are being manipulated—"

"Enough!" snapped Blighttongue. "Will you provide a stenographer to take Mr. Wildeye's confession, or shall I have him write it out longhand and send it to The Covenancy Today for immediate publication?"

"Don't do this, Mr. Wildeye," Sam urged. "Don't throw your life away to protect a gang of thugs."

Wildeye bristled. "You know nothing, McCoy. *Nothing!*"

With a sigh, Sam shook his head. Then he stood and went to the door to call for a stenographer.

11

Adam sat behind his desk, feet propped up on the top of it, reading glasses perched on the tip of his nose. His eyes flicked back and forth as he read Wildeye's confession, his frown growing grimmer and grimmer. When he finished the last page, he slapped the sheaf of papers to his desk and swept his reading glasses up to the crown of his head, rubbing his temples with one thumb and finger, palm covering his eyes. "What a mess," he said.

"Yeah," said Sam. "He's insulated the GC completely."

"What I can't figure out is why... Ivtavin is young—well, for a goblin—and has a wife and children. Why throw all that away to protect a man who's busy throwing him under the bus in the Covenancy media?" asked Angie. "Why is he so loyal?"

Sam frowned. "I prosecuted a Redcap almost twenty years ago, now. He stuck to the most ludicrous story I've ever heard. He claimed sole responsibility for a rash of robberies across the City. Closed-circuit cameras caught three of the bank robberies, you see, and while only his face was visible, there were clearly four other goblins in those banks. He insisted those images were illusory, or sometimes he claimed they were camera malfunctions. The point is, he took the whole rap."

Angie shook her head. "Why?"

"His family lives like royalty to this day," said Sam. "And to be honest, though he's in the dungeon under Sing Sing, he lives almost as well as his family. It was his sacrifice for the clan, you see? And the Redcaps reward sacrifice."

"Then Ivtavin Wildeye—"

"Is doing this to provide for his loved ones. His life is over, regardless of whether he takes the rap or not, and if he turns on those higher up in the clan, his family will become pariahs—shunned, outcast, left to starve, if they're even left alive."

"Witness Protection?"

Sam shook his head, lips pursed. "In my experience, goblins won't go for the whole new identity thing."

Adam dropped his feet to the floor and looked up at her. "Sometimes, you have to be satisfied with what you can get."

Angie frowned. "More and more, it seems like the wrong people are getting the long sentences, while the really bad actors get to go home and kiss their loved ones and celebrate."

"No one said the justice system was perfect," murmured Sam.

"No, but I thought it was better than this."

"We take what we can get," said Adam. "Then we move on to the next case."

"And sometimes," Sam said with a twinkle in his eye, "the press gets hold of a story."

"What was that?" asked Adam, his back to them as he put away the decanter of Glenlivet. "I didn't hear that last part."

12

The Covenancy Today's headline fairly shouted from the newsstands—one-hundred-twenty-point type and even an exclamation mark—"GRAND CYNOSURE SLYPINCH IMPLICATED IN REDCAP SCHEME!" The online aggregators bounced the headline across everyone's feed with equal parts outrage and lunatic excitement. Pundits on both sides made cartloads of money pontificating about laws they didn't understand, about evidence they'd never seen, suppositions flying as thick as snow in a blizzard. In other words, everything was normal in the next day's news cycle.

Sam met Angie on the courthouse steps, grinning and carrying a copy of The Covenancy Today, carefully folded to show the headline. She grinned at him as he approached. "I heard they're calling for impeachment," she said, dimples flashing.

Sam sobered a mite. "Don't get your hopes up, Angie. There have been something like eighty impeachments brought by the Hearth, but only twenty have made it through to the Conclave. And of those twenty, only eight have been convicted—and none of those had a higher rank than Covenancy Judge."

Her smile faltered. "Then...why?" She lifted a helpless hand at the headline.

"It was never about getting the GC impeached," said Sam. He flipped the paper over, pointed to a story below the fold, and read its title. "Election Oversight Committee Announces Increased Scrutiny of the GC's Re-election Campaign Practices. Sometimes Lady Justice acts behind the scenes." He pointed to another story and read, "GC's Approval Rating the Lowest on Record—All Initiatives on Hold."

Angie nodded. "It's not dungeon time, though."

"No," said Sam. "But for the GC, this might be worse." He glanced down at his watch. "Speaking of dungeons, let's go make sure Ivtavin Wildeye gets as much time as possible."

They turned and climbed the rest of the steps smiling secret smiles.

CHAPTER 4

THE VERDICT

I

The gallery was standing room only as Leery and Dru slipped in the back. Angie and Sam already sat at their customary table, and on the other side of the aisle sat an ugly goblin in a beautiful Italian wool suit. "The place is a madhouse," whispered Leery. "You wouldn't think there'd be this much attention over a case like this."

Dru cocked her head to the side and stared at him.

"What? Is my tie on funny again?"

She shook her head. "I get that you pretend you can't use technology, Oriscoe, but you do read the papers, right?"

"Well..."

"Come on, I've seen them on your desk."

Leery shrugged. "Coffee rings."

"I can't quite tell if this is part of your endearing aw-shucks act."

He grinned down at her. "I'll never tell."

"I could make you tell me," she said with a mischievous twinkle in her eye. Then she smiled, and for Leery, the rest of the world ceased to exist.

He took half a step toward her, then swallowed convulsively. "Uh...turn down the wattage a little? I'm not made of stone, you know."

She let him ride the lightning for a moment longer, then wrinkled her nose at him. "But I guess I'll have to be satisfied with making you look at me that way." She winked. "At least for now."

"For...now," he whispered huskily. "Yeah."

Hermann of Wied, Judge Agrippa's bailiff, appeared next to them, a knowing grin on his lips. "Might I suggest standing farther apart? Perhaps the length of the Bible would suit?"

"Sorry, Your Cardinal-ness," said Leery. "The devil made her do it."

Hermann disappeared behind his benign smile and reappeared in the center of the courtroom. He cleared his throat and banged his ghostly crozier against the floorboard soundlessly. "Hear ye, hear ye," he almost-sang in a buttery voice. "Attend ye and pay homage to his August Honor, Heinrich Cornelius Agrippa."

The courtroom filled with the clatter of everyone standing and murmuring to one another. Then, the door behind the bench banged open and Agrippa marched into the room, his cold, dead glare zipping from the prosecution table to the defense. He mounted the bench and reached for his gavel, but it slipped from his fingers with a rattle. He stared down at it as if the thing offended him, then dismissed it with a wave of his hand. "I call this proceeding to order!" He glared at the defense magister. "Am I to understand that your client wishes to plead guilty? That he is prepared to allocute to his crimes in full? Am I further to understand that he has no sentencing agreement with the Prosecutor? And no plea bargain?"

Blighttongue stood. "Yes, Your Honor. You have the right of it."

"Most unusual...uh..."

"Fizhauk Blighttongue, Your Honor. Of the firm Blighttongue, Brightflame, and Grumpneck."

"Doesn't sound familiar," mumbled Agrippa.

"No, Judge, it should not. We practice mostly at the seat of government, though I maintain my bar credentials here in the Big Apple."

"Uh, yes," murmured Agrippa. "In Washington D.C., you say?"

"Yes, Your Honor."

Agrippa tilted his head to the side. "Most unusual, though all appears in order." He turned a marble-eyed stare at Ivtavin Wildeye. "And you. Mr. Wildeye, is it?"

Wildeye stood. "Yes, Your Honor."

"You realize that I am under no constraint in handing down your sentence? That I can sentence you to the maximum for each and every count?"

"Yes, Judge," said Wildeye, though he looked a little green around the gills.

"And the charges, Mr. Wildeye…" Agrippa shook his head. "Numerous counts of conspiracy to defraud, conspiracy to extort a public official, misuse of campaign funds, conspiracy to manufacture and distribute controlled substances, and twenty-four counts of conspiracy to commit magical murder. Are you aware I may sentence you to in excess of twenty-four lifetimes?"

"Yes, Your Honor," said the goblin. "I only wish to accelerate this interminable waiting and begin serving my sentence."

"Well…" Agrippa leaned back and squinted down at him. "I simply can't overlook the potential, uh, conflict of interest of your magister. Are you aware that his firm also represents the GC?"

"Yes. None of that matters."

"Does it not?" asked Agrippa, arching an eyebrow to incredible heights. "I shouldn't have to counsel you on this, sir, but my conscious dictates I must. You have many options to mitigate your sentence. For one, you could negotiate an agreement with the prosecution in order to reduce your sentence."

"I know that, Your Honor," said Wildeye, failing to meet the judge's stare. "I still want to plead guilty. I've done wrong, and I should pay for that."

Agrippa flicked his gaze to Sam, who shrugged. "Are you aware that you may not appeal a conviction based on your admissions?"

"Yes, Your Honor," said Ivtavin.

With a glance toward Hermann of Wied, Agrippa nodded. "Then who am I to stand in your way? Please begin your allocution."

"Right," said Wildeye. "I worked as Grand Cynosure Slypinch's campaign manager. During the course of the campaign, as well as since, I diverted campaign monies to a special bank account I'd set up with Klignas Findfault. The money paid for special projects Findfault undertook on my behalf. Snacks. Moving the Unknown—the militant arm of the otherwise benign Redcap organization—into Manhattan proper. Sometimes that last one required...certain..."

"Come, come!" snapped Agrippa. "No disseminations."

"Sometimes they killed people to make the move easier. Or to confuse the police. Or to protect the snacks. Whatever. I did it all on my own, without anyone else involved. I'm guilty of the charges you read." He shrugged. "That's it."

Agrippa leaned forward and squinted down at him. "And the Grand Cynosure's involvement?"

"As I said, I did it on my own."

"That seems unlikely, sir," said Agrippa with a sigh. "Are you, too, a Redcap?"

"I am," said Wildeye after a nod from Blighttongue.

"And a member of this Unknown group?"

"Yes."

"And is the Grand Cynosure?"

"Your Honor, surely—"

"I'll hear no more from you, Mr. Blighttongue, if you please."

Blighttongue smiled, but at the same time, he looked as though he'd just swallowed a pint of urine.

"Mr. Wildeye? Answer my question."

"Your Honor, the GC has publicly renounced his affiliation with the Redcaps."

"Well, I know that, don't I? Was Fidonk Slypinch a member of this Unknown you spoke of?"

"I... Membership is secret, Your Honor."

"Then did you ever see Fidonk Slypinch at any Unknown functions, meetings, or events? Ever speak to the man about it?"

"He admitted to being a Redcap, Your Honor, but—"

"Answer me!" Agrippa's voice cracked like a whip. "Is Slypinch an active member of the Redcaps?"

"Yes!" snapped Wildeye. "You can't leave the Redcaps, no matter what you say."

Agrippa nodded. "And is your magister also a member?"

"I am, Your Honor. Many goblins are. Many are born into the organization, and there is nothing illegal or immoral about being a member. It is a misunderstood—"

"Fine. Are you, Blighttongue, a member of the Unknown?"

"No!"

"And is the GC?" Agrippa demanded of Wildeye, again.

"I'm directing my client not to answer," said Blighttongue. "You overstep, Your Honor!"

"That's answer enough, is it not?" asked the judge in a mild tone. "Mr. Wildeye, do you expect this court to believe that you undertook this business with the Unknown without the GC's approval?"

"I'm directing my client to refrain from answering that question and any other you ask about His Excellency, the Grand Cynosure."

"And if I were to offer your client a suspended sentence? Would he still remain silent?"

Wildeye squeezed his eyes shut, then said, "I would, Your Honor."

"Very well!" snapped Agrippa. "I have tried, Mr. Wildeye, to act in your interests, but it seems you are not moved by my arguments. I accept your guilty plea and am ready to pronounce sentence. For each count of conspiracy to commit murder, I sentence you to one lifetime plus fifteen years. For the charge of conspiracy to defraud, I sentence you to five years. On the charge of conspiracy to extort a public official, I sentence you to two years. On the charge of misuse of campaign funds, once again I impose a sentence of two and one-half years. All sentences will be served *consecutively*, Mr. Wildeye, since you are uncooperative in applying justice to the guilty. All told, the butcher's bill is twenty-four lifetimes plus three-hundred-sixty-nine-and-one-half years, served in a facility designated by the Locus of New York's Department of Corrections." He fumbled at his gavel for a few moments, then snapped, "So ordered! Bailiff, take the defendant and convey him into the custody of the DOC." He spun and stomped through the door leading to his chambers.

"Well, I guess that's it, then," Leery said in Dru's ear. "Coffee?"

CHAPTER 5

THE END

I

Adam got up and went over to his decanter of scotch. "You've had a couple of klinkers lined up in a row," he said while he got out two glasses and began to pour. "You are understandably discouraged, Angie, but your track record is pretty good, and Sam positively glows when he speaks of you. No, you didn't get the GC, but it was unrealistic to expect that."

"It disgusts me," said Angie. "I..." She swallowed hard. "I've had another offer."

Adam grimaced and handed her a tumbler of Glenlivet. "His Excellency?"

"I..." Angie blushed. "Well, yes, since you already know. He's asked me to head up his legal team."

Adam nodded. "It's a good opportunity."

"That's it?" asked Angie.

With a smile and a shrug, Adam nodded. "It *is* a good opportunity. Lucifer's interests are vast, and he'll keep you busy. Of that, there's no doubt."

"But..."

"But there's a lot of boring contract work, Angie. And you have that killer instinct required to become a great prosecutor. You see to the heart of the matter more often than not. I think you'll be bored."

Angie grimaced down at her scotch, then swilled it in a circle and took a sip. "I'd miss the scotch, that's for sure."

Adam chuckled. "If you're going to head up a legal department, you'd better get used to buying crates of the stuff. I can give you the name of a great distributor." He sobered. "If you decide to go, Angie, you will be missed."

She lifted her chin and flashed a flat smile. "Thanks, Adam."

"Think about it," he urged.

"I…" She nodded. "I will. It seems like every time I think I've decided, I change my mind."

"You'll always be welcome here," said Adam, toasting her with his tumbler. "No matter what you decide."

2

Leery and Dru were the last to arrive, and as they filed into the LM's filled, but silent, conference room, their smiles faded. "What?" asked Leery as he pulled out a chair for Dru.

"This was hand-delivered before the office opened this morning," said Adam. He grimaced and threw a copy of The Covenancy Today in the middle of the table. The huge headline announced a recent vote of no confidence and a mutual announcement from both the Hearth and the Conclave stating their intent to act in concert to block the GC's initiatives and calling for his resignation.

"Hey, that's good news, isn't it?" He glanced at the faces arrayed around the table. Sam sucked his teeth and stared down at the table in front of him. Angie nodded but didn't look happy at all. Ice Cofy puffed out his cheeks, while Dawn sat with her eyes closed.

"It came with this note," said Adam, and he spun a piece of eight-by-ten cardstock after the paper. Scrawled across the page in either the same flowing calligraphic script as the note to Alentina Washburn or one so close as not to matter, was the single line: "We pay what we owe."

Leery arched his eyebrow. "Redcaps, eh?"

Adam shrugged. "It would appear so, but as you can see, it's unsigned."

"A threat," said Dru.

"Yeah, but what idiot would think it's a good idea to threaten a bunch of cops and magisters?" asked Cofy.

"A group of criminals used to getting what they want in everything they do," murmured Sam. "An ages-old organization that's stood in plain sight for centuries, doing as they please...and getting away with it."

"So, what? We're supposed to be scared by this little love letter?" asked Leery, sneering down at the paper. "I'm a cop, and you're the LM, Adam. Making enemies is in our DNA. I can't see quitting over this."

"No," said Adam. "But you'd be a fool to ignore it. You've all got targets painted on your backs. To what extent, I can't say, but you need to be careful. Don't take foolish risks." His graze crawled up to meet Leery's.

"Hey, I agree completely," said Leery. "From now on, no more tuna fish sandwiches."

I hope you've enjoyed this episode of CLAW & WARDER and are clawing at the door to get on to the next. *A Tail of Two Cities: CLAW & WARDER Episode 7* can be found here: https://ehv4.us/4cw7.

If you've enjoyed this novel, please consider joining my Readers Group by visiting https://ehv4.us/join. Or follow me on BookBub by visiting my profile page there: https://ehv4.us/bbub.

For my complete bibliography, please visit: https://ehv4.us/bib.

Books these days succeed or fail based on the strength of their reviews. I hope you will consider leaving a review—as an independent author, I could use your help. It's easy (I promise). You can leave your review by clicking on this link: https://ehv4.us/2revcw6.

AUTHOR'S NOTE

Every time I reach the end of a novel, I experience a rush of emotions. Joy, accomplishment, and a kind of giddy expectation—waiting to hear whether readers have enjoyed the book—but also a sense of loss, of sadness that the story is over.

This novel is a little different, and if you read the dedication, you already know why.

I had a tough time bringing this story to a close, not only because I found it difficult to write humor while mourning the loss of my nephew, but also because I almost didn't want it to end. And then there's Mr. Story, who read my mood and kept trying to turn this into a serious story with a grim ending.

I hope I've beaten Mr. Story back, that I've entertained you, and despite my grief, that I've made you laugh. I learn things about myself with each new book, and this book helped me learn how much I *want* to make people laugh. How much I want to lighten their load, even if only for a moment. In many ways, I tend to write that desire into my characters, my leading men especially.

I must admit that I love writing about Dru and Leery. I like their relationship, and like in the Blood of the Isir series, I see a lot of the relationship Supergirl and I share in it. Their easy banter, sure, but also the way they just seem to fit together to make something better than they can make separately. Call me a romantic, call me a lunatic...

I'm good with either.

I wish you all the best, my friend, and I wish you many, many smiles, giggles, and even a few guffaws until we meet this way again.

ABOUT THE AUTHOR

Erik Henry Vick is an author of dark speculative fiction who writes despite a disability caused by his Personal Monster™ (also known as an autoimmune disease.) He writes to hang on to the few remaining shreds of his sanity.

He lives in Western New York with his wife, Supergirl; their son; a Rottweiler named after a god of thunder; and two extremely psychotic cats. He fights his Personal Monster™ daily with humor, pain medicine, and funny T-shirts.

Erik has a B.A. in Psychology, an M.S.C.S., and a Ph.D. in Artificial Intelligence. He has worked as a criminal investigator for a state agency, a college professor, a C.T.O. for an international software company, and a video game developer.

He'd love to hear from you on social media:

Blog: https://erikhenryvick.com
Twitter: https://twitter.com/BerserkErik
Facebook: https://fb.me/erikhenryvick
Amazon author pages:
    USA: https://ehv4.us/amausa
    UK: https://ehv4.us/amauk
Goodreads Author Page: https://ehv4.us/gr
BookBub Author Profile: http://ehv4.us/bbub

Made in the USA
Monee, IL
29 January 2023